SAVING
ARM
PIT

Published in Canada by Fitzhenry & Whiteside, 195 Allstate Parkway, Markham, Ontario L3R 4T8

Published in the United States by Fitzhenry & Whiteside, 311 Washington Street, Brighton, Massachusetts 02135

www.fitzhenry.ca godwit@fitzhenry.ca

10 9 8 7 6 5 4

Library and Archives Canada Cataloguing in Publication
Hyde, Natalie, 1963-
Saving Armpit / Natalie Hyde.
ISBN 978-1-55455-151-4
I. Title.
PS8615.Y44S29 2011   j813'.6   C2011-901398-3

Publisher Cataloging-in-Publication Data (U.S)
Hyde, Natalie.
Saving Armpit / Natalie Hyde.
[136] p. : 12.7 x 19.05 cm.
ISBN: 978-1-55455-151-4 (pbk.)
1. Baseball – Juvenile fiction. 2. Community life – Juvenile fiction. I. Title.
[F] dc22   PZ7.H934Sa 2011

Fitzhenry & Whiteside acknowledges with thanks the Canada Council for the Arts, and the Ontario Arts Council for their support of our publishing program. We acknowledge the financial support of the Government of Canada through the Book Publishing Industry Development Program (BPIDP) for our publishing activities.

Cover and interior design by Kerry Designs
Cover image by Ted Heeley
Printed in Canada

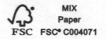

MIX
Paper
FSC FSC® C004071

SAVING
ARM
PIT

Natalie Hyde

Fitzhenry & Whiteside
www.fitzhenry.ca

Acknowledgements:

It turns out that writing a book is a team sport, too.

A heartfelt thanks to all the Kidcritters who gave such
wonderful feedback on this manuscript. Special thanks to
the gang at Summer Writing Workshops who helped me
brainstorm the title.

Thank you also to Patricia Lee Gauch, who worked with me
on an early draft of this story.

I would also like to thank everyone at Fitzhenry & Whiteside
for the wonderful job they did bringing this story to life,
especially my editor, Christie Harkin, for her wonderful
suggestions, her warmth and her great sense of humour.

Most of all I wish to thank Craig, Alex, Chelsey, Nathan
and Haley for pinch-hitting with the chores when I had a
deadline looming. Your love and encouragement mean the
world to me.

For Chelsey, my first reader

I gripped the bat with clammy hands. It was the bottom of the last inning and the pitcher for the Bulldogs had a nasty drop-curve ball that would home in on my shin like a cruise missile. I was still limping from the last time I came up to bat against him. It was a great motivator. Either hit the ball or be crippled.

The pitcher pulled back his arm and released the ball.

I jumped back from home plate with both feet as the ball whistled past my knees.

"Strike!"

I shook my head and tried to concentrate. The pitcher was grinning. I was sweating.

"Come on, Clay! The next one has your name on it." I know Scott meant to say that I was going to hit the ball and not be hit *by* it, but part of me worried my best friend had just jinxed me.

It would feel so good to connect with the ball and send it screaming out into left field so hard it would wipe the smirks right off the Bulldogs' faces. We were down two to nothing and I was tired of our team being a joke in the league. A filler. You know—a team to practice on in between the important games. Out of the corner of my eye, I could see the Bulldogs all leaning on the fence in front of their dugout, snickering.

"Bring me home, Clay." Stewy was on third, which was something of a miracle. He was a great hitter but not a great runner. He could really put his weight behind the bat and send the ball flying, which would usually buy him enough time to make it to first. But that was about it. And when he did go, he didn't exactly run; *lumbering* is more what you'd call the way he moved. It was only because of some wild throws and the fact that no one could understand Coach Meyers's signals that he now stood on third, arms folded.

A big hit here and we could tie the game.

I planted my feet in the dirt and sucked in my breath as I waited for the next pitch. What I wouldn't give to end the Terriers' losing streak, to know how it felt to win! It wasn't a feeling I was familiar with—or something any other team expected from us, coming from the losing-est town in history.

The pitcher playfully tossed the ball up and down a few times. Then he looked at me with a glint in his eye and went into his wind-up.

He threw the ball with a grunt. I saw it coming straight at my head. I dropped like a stone to avoid a concussion. The catcher missed the ball and scrambled up from his squat to chase it.

Coach Meyers yelled at Stewy to steal home.

Our whole bench froze. Stewy was *never* called on to steal. You know, the lumbering and all that. But Coach was screaming now and Stewy was nothing if not a team player. So he started moving, his legs pounding, his arms pumping.

I stepped back from the plate and shook my head. Mr. Meyers was nice enough to volunteer time as the Terriers' coach but he knew nothing—*nothing*—about baseball.

The catcher was in no hurry to get the ball at first, but when he looked over his shoulder as he bent to pick it up, he saw a locomotive chugging toward home.

Now that Stewy was moving, everyone on our bench was up and yelling for him. The catcher grabbed the ball and ran back to tag him.

"Dive! Dive!" screamed Coach Meyers.

There was only one second's confusion on Stewy's face before he threw his arms in front of him and went headfirst toward home plate.

Stewy lifted his dust-covered face and spit out a mouthful of dirt. He was still ten inches away from the plate and the catcher was standing over him with a smug look on his face. I didn't even *know* the guy and I didn't like him.

"Out!" barked the umpire. Then he signaled with his arms that that was the third out. The game was over.

The Bulldogs cheered and high-fived each other.

So much for a big hit saving the day.

It was a stupid hope, anyway. Our town didn't have its reputation for nothing. All the teams lost: the curling team, the Old Timers' Hockey League—even our barbershop quartet. Why should the Terriers be any different?

And now this. Our third loss this season. It didn't sound so bad until you realized it was only the third game. And it was the twenty-third consecutive loss, if you started counting two years ago.

I helped Stewy up. "I think Coach meant to say 'slide', Stewy."

"Yeah, shlide," Stewy said spitting out more dirt. "I shoulda shlid."

As we got near the bench, the team ran over to us, laughing and thumping Stewy on the back.

"Now that's what I call losing with style!" Scott punched my arm with a big grin. "And you, my friend, got through the game with both shins intact. You have to admit, this was our best loss yet!"

I tried to smile but the words stung. *Best loss yet?* Did Harmony lose often so that now we had to rank our losses?

If you ask me, there is no place better to live than Harmony Point. Me and the guys spend the better part of the summer tearing around the fields or building forts in the woods. In the spring, we have raft races down Bluffton

Creek and in the winter we "borrow" the inner tubes off of Stewy's dad's tractor and whip down the hills that surround our town. Only the bravest of us jump off the point that got our town its name. It is a huge rock that juts out from the top of the bluffs and I've jumped it twice, even though my stomach felt like it was up in my throat.

You can't do stuff like that in the city, you know. The "city" is really called Holmesville, just over the bluffs, but to me it's just one big concrete octopus spreading its giant sucker arms, reaching out and trying to swallow our town.

It was bad enough having the city take over our police and fire departments and even exchanging our mayor for a seat on the Holmesville city council last year, but to my mind, losing our name was the sorest point.

On April Fools' Day, some stupid vandals had spray-painted out a few key letters on our HARMONY POINT town sign so it now read ARM P I T. My ears went red every time I saw it.

It was like we were a place that should stay tucked away or avoided. Like we were an embarrassment for the nearby city. I had to wonder what we would lose next.

I didn't have long to wait.

It's a Retirement Party!

AFTER MANY YEARS OF SERVICE,
(SHE WON'T LET US SAY HOW
MANY!)

MRS. JEAN STANFIELD

IS RETIRING AS POSTMISTRESS
OF HARMONY POINT.

WE ARE HAVING A RECEPTION IN
THE POST OFFICE
TO CELEBRATE AND WISH HER
WELL IN HER RETIREMENT!

JOIN US ON
SATURDAY, MAY 16
2 PM TO 4 PM

EVERYONE WELCOME!

REFRESHMENTS COURTESY OF
MISS APFELBAUM

I couldn't believe it when I heard Mrs. Stanfield was retiring. She had worked in the village post office forever. Picking up the mail wasn't such a chore because I always knew there was a mint waiting for me in her corked glass jar sitting on the counter. And if I wasted some time and pretended to look at the notice board, I heard all the juicy news. Everyone told Mrs. Stanfield everything. She was kinda like the town shrink. I would learn the most amazing things while reading about Abelson's livestock auction or the First Aid course being offered at the Legion.

I overheard the news that the mystery of the vanishing laundry had finally been solved. Mr. Williams saw Doug Scupton's goat running loose under Mrs. Dorset's clothesline two days earlier, with something red and lacy dangling from its mouth. He swore he was going to bill Doug for two pairs of long underwear that had disappeared from his own clothesline last week.

And Mrs. Stanfield almost had to break up a riot in the post office when Mrs. Danforth told Mrs. Morgan that the committee wanted to move the Strawberry Social from the last week in June to the second week in July.

That's even how I met my best friend. Well, he wasn't actually *in* the post office, but that's where I was when I heard the real estate lady telling Mrs. Stanfield about the new family that had bought the old Sutton place right next to ours. When Mrs. Stanfield asked her what kind of people they were, the real estate lady lowered her voice. I moved closer because that's when you hear all the good stuff.

She told her that they were kinda nerdy science-types who spent all their time in the lab at the university. They were worried about their son and thought they could give him a more normal childhood by bringing him to a small town. I don't know how "normal" Harmony Point is, but it sure is better than living in the city, and that's a fact.

I checked him out the next day, wondering how he would take the ribbing all newbies get. It's harmless, really. But we have a good laugh watching them go to the hardware store looking for the special "dirt-road bike-chain oil" or checking the culverts for the rare "ankle-biting opossum." Scott seemed kind of quiet and serious and I didn't want him to get the wrong idea about us, so I stuck by him and clued him in. Scott and I have barely been apart since.

Saturday afternoon, we walked over to Mrs. Stanfield's retirement party at the post office together—the whole village was going. The ancient red brick building sat hunched right by the road with barely enough room for a sidewalk. It must have been a pretty important building at one time. It was a full two stories high and had lots of those windows with little wavy windowpanes. I heard it used to be a stagecoach stop before it was a telegraph office and then a post office. The square concrete trough that still stands across the street was where they watered the horses, although now it just holds some droopy geraniums.

"If more than two hundred people come today," Scott said to me, "that would be a turnout of over sixty percent."

"What is it with you and numbers?" I asked for the millionth time. Scott has a total math brain. He can come up with facts and figures that would put Statistics Canada to shame.

Scott shrugged his bony shoulders. "I bet you don't get sixty percent of *city* residents out to a retirement party," he said.

"No way," I agreed, trying to figure out sixty percent of 135,000. "That would be..."

"81,000," Scott said, without even thinking hard.

"Yeah, 81,000 people. I don't see it happening."

"Besides, we have cake," Scott said.

I stared at him. Sometimes Scott had really crazy ideas. "You think people care more when there's dessert?"

"Hey, this ain't no ordinary cake. It's an *Apfelbaum*."

"Oh, well that explains it then," I said, rolling my eyes.

"I'm just saying," Scott said, shrugging again, "there's *cake*."

The wood-panelled post office smelled of ink and musty papers. The noise grew louder as people elbowed each other and stepped on each other's toes to get to the refreshments. Everyone *ooh*ed and *aah*ed as Miss Apfelbaum brought in the cake.

"So what's the deal with everyone trying to marry Miss Apfelbaum off?" Scott asked me.

Sometimes it's hard for me to explain village politics to him. Especially when I don't really understand them myself.

"I don't know. I think maybe married women can't stand to see someone happily single."

Scott raised his eyebrows. "So, do you think she will? Get married, I mean?"

"Mom says by the time you're middle aged, it's pretty slim pickings."

"Well, I don't see what the big deal is, anyway."

I agreed with him. Miss Apfelbaum was one of the most cheerful people I knew. She always had time to help out around town, whether it was with the Legion's bake sale or the Horticultural Club's spring planting. Stewy said people *change* when they get married. I sorta hoped it would never happen; I liked Miss Apfelbaum the way she was.

She set the enormous cake on the counter that was covered with a vinyl picnic tablecloth. Little cocktail napkins with the words "Way to Go!" were stacked beside small Styrofoam plates and plastic forks. I don't want to say that our town is cheap—we don't get the kind of funding the city does—but sometimes I gotta wonder who comes up with these ideas.

"*Way to Go!* napkins? Couldn't they even spring for *Happy Retirement* napkins?" I asked. "These look like they're left over from the last Terriers' championship party."

"Don't be stupid, Clay," Scott said. "The Terriers haven't won the Championship in what—eighty years or something? Those napkins would have disintegrated by now. Besides, I think it's funny."

It was kinda funny. But I didn't feel like laughing. You know, I almost didn't take a piece at all. I didn't want to celebrate Mrs. Stanfield leaving. I would miss her. I doubted the new postman would give out mints and collect all the news. I sighed but picked up a plate, fork, and *Way to Go!* napkin anyway. I couldn't bring myself to lose out on a piece of an Apfelbaum cake.

Miss Apfelbaum's cakes were famous. Well, around here, anyway. They were huge and had real whipped cream—not that spray stuff that disappears as soon as you put it in your mouth.

This one looked awesome. The counter was barely wide enough to hold the layers and layers of cake battling for space with the cream and strawberries. The whole thing looked like an envelope with Mrs. Stanfield's new address in Fredericton, New Brunswick, written in icing in the middle. More icing spelled "Postage Due" in red across the front, and up in the right-hand corner was an icing stamp. It looked so real I thought it was a photograph. It was an Apfelbaum masterpiece.

"Hey, isn't that Elvis?" Scott asked, pointing at the stamp.

"I want the piece with Elvis on it," I told Stewy's mom who stood behind the counter cutting the cake.

"That's not Elvis," she said. "That's Barry Manilow." She leaned over as she slid the wedge of cake onto my plate. "Miss Apfelbaum has had a crush on him since the day she first heard 'Mandy'."

"Who's Barry Manilow?" Scott whispered to me as we squeezed out of the post office to sit outside on the stone retaining wall across the street.

I shrugged, taking a bite of cake. "Don't know, but he sure tastes good."

"Did you hear Coach Meyers quit?" Scott mumbled unexpectedly, crumbs falling from his mouth.

I almost choked on Barry Manilow. Mrs. Stanfield wasn't even out the door and already we had lost something else.

"No! Why'd he quit?"

"I guess he was pretty mad when Stewy showed up at the last game in his dad's scuba gear."

I didn't mean to laugh. I mean, I wasn't happy we had lost our coach. But it really had been a sight to see Stewy decked out like that.

"Stewy was going to be ready the next time Coach told him to 'dive'," I said and we both broke out into peals of laughter again. But then the laughs died in my throat. "What about the team?" I asked.

"Don't know," Scott said. "Maybe we'll have to fold for this year and join the Holmesville league next year."

I could feel my stomach twist into a pretzel. Join the *city* league? No way. But with no coach, how were we ever going to keep our team and prove that we weren't just a bunch of losers?

Harmony Point Elementary School

P. A. DAY REMINDER!

May 14, 20-

To All Parents:

This is a reminder that Monday, May 18th is a P.A. Day!

It seems there must have been some confusion on the last P.A. day as some parents tried to send their children to school anyway. Please be advised that although our janitor, Mr. Medeiros, enjoyed the donuts, tarts and homemade apple cider, he will *not* be able to unlock the doors for them this time.

Our teachers will be spending the day taking courses and attending seminars including "Monday Morning Panic Attacks" and "Countdown to Summer Vacation." I'm sure they will be back on Tuesday with renewed enthusiasm. Hopefully, their new skills will help them redirect all that springtime exuberance in their classrooms into productive energy.

Enjoy an extra day with your children!

Yours respectfully,

Janet Barnes
Principal Janet Barnes

S cott and I were sitting on the stone wall trying to think of something cool to do on our P.A. day. We were just deciding between sliding down the grassy bluffs on big pieces of cardboard and hanging ropes in the trees in Bluffton Park so we could swing through them like Tarzan, when the new postman arrived. We sat for a while and watched as just about every lady from the village went in and out of the post office like it had a revolving door.

On our way home for lunch after a wild session of bluff surfing, we saw the postman stagger out the door again, looking a little dazed. And it was no wonder. I heard my mom tell Scott's mom that in just under four hours—a village record I think—they had learned all about him. Stuff like Mr. Blackmore was a widower in his fifties with two grown children, he never ironed, he loved to cook Italian food, and he was a Gemini. Who cared about that? What got my attention was that not only had they roped him into donating to St. Ursula's garage sale and calling the next two bingo games in the church hall, but he was also taking over as coach of the

Harmony Terriers baseball team.

"Do you think he knows anything about baseball?" Scott asked.

"How much could a postman know about baseball?" I said, not wanting to get my hopes up. I had already resigned myself to the prospect of another year of losing.

"Still, he can't be much worse than the last one," Scott said. "I mean, Coach Meyers kept telling me to hit the ball with my 'club.' How bad can this guy be?"

I had to agree. Still, would he be good enough to help us to win a game?

"Do you think we can beat the Pirates on Saturday?" I asked, glad that our regular Wednesday night game had been cancelled. I figured it would be better if our new coach got used to us not catching balls in practice before we did it in a real game. Kinda break him in slowly.

"Nah. They're three-and-O this season."

There he went, talking to me in numbers again.

"Not to mention they got a real coach, cool uniforms, and even new aluminum bats."

"Yeah," I said, my hopes sinking again. "We don't even have shirts all the same colour green."

"And we have two number eights."

"Isn't that illegal in baseball?"

"Doesn't matter. Neither one got a hit last year anyway."

Mr. Blackmore was late for his first Terriers' practice Thursday after school. When he showed up at Bluffton Park dragging a huge navy sports bag, we were hanging upside down from the dome climber and twirling on the baby swings, gloves and hats scattered everywhere. But when he started pulling equipment out of the bag, it drew us like moths to a porch light. Out came a catcher's mask that wasn't all scratched and bent, shin pads with all the buckles, a chest protector with a lower part that protected more than your chest (if you know what I mean), and at least four different-sized bats.

"Where'd you get all this?" Stewy asked, "Did you rob the hardware store?" Stewy was never shy about saying what was on his mind.

Coach Blackmore blinked behind his wire-frame glasses. "No. This was my son's equipment."

"You mean you actually *know* something about baseball?" Stewy asked, his eyebrows raised.

Coach Blackmore gave a small smile. "Well, a little. So, who plays what position here?"

"We don't have no positions," Tim said, shaking his frizzy hair.

"We don't have *any* positions," Tom corrected his twin,

his identical mop stuffed under a cap.

"That's what I said."

"No, you didn't. You used a double negative."

"Did not. What's a double negative?"

One of the twins' famous arguments was about to erupt. I sat back down on the freshly mowed grass to wait it out.

"Isn't a double negative when you can't go to trial for the same crime twice?" Stewy asked, egging them on. He loved a good fight.

"Nah, that's double *jeopardy*," Tom scoffed.

"Stupid. Double jeopardy is when the money is higher and the questions are tougher," Tim said.

"You're thinking of *final jeopardy*, dingbat." Tom swatted Tim with the back of his hand.

Tim jumped up, his hands in tight fists. "Is that your *final answer*, smart mouth?"

"Different show," his brother taunted him, getting to his feet.

"Gentlemen, gentlemen!" Coach Blackmore held up his hands, palms out. "Baseball, remember?" The boys sat down on the grass again, glowering. I was kinda glad he stopped them when he did. Left on their own, the twins' arguments almost always ended in a brawl.

"Now, who played first base last year?"

All ten of us put our hands up. Coach Blackmore looked puzzled.

"Okay. Who played shortstop?"

All ten hands stayed up. Worry began to creep over his face.

"Catcher?" His voice grew weaker.

No one put their hand down.

"Pitcher?" He was almost squeaking now.

"I told you. We didn't have no positions," Tim glared at his twin, daring him to argue. "We all played everything. Coach Meyers just mixed us up every inning."

Coach Blackmore sagged visibly. "Batting order?" He almost whispered.

"Shortest to tallest," Sophie answered. She was the only girl on the team but we didn't mind her. She could outrun all of us in a sprint.

"So," Coach Blackmore said slowly. "We need to start from the beginning then." He managed a weak smile and wiped sweat from his brow even though it was a cool May afternoon.

The first thing he made us do was throw the ball back and forth with a partner. Every time one of us caught the ball, we were supposed to both take one step back. If one of us dropped the ball, then we had to start over.

Coach Blackmore promised a pack of gum to the first pair that made it twenty steps apart. Balls were flying everywhere. It's harder than it looks, you know. After about twenty minutes with no winners in sight, he just gave us each a piece.

Batting practice was next. Coach Blackmore squatted beside home plate and gently lobbed the ball for us to hit. I loved the satisfying *thwack* of the bat hitting the ball. Especially since I didn't hear it very often.

"You've got a nice swing there, Clay," Coach Blackmore told me. "Just keep the bat level." I managed a couple of *thwacks*.

When Stewy went up for his turn at bat, everyone automatically moved back.

The very first ball went flying straight up into the air.

"I've got it," called three voices at the same time. Sophie sprinted over from third base just as Tim and Tom raced in from the outfield.

Three gloves were open to the sky. The ball fell on the ground between them.

"Let's just have one person get those pop flies, okay?" Coach Blackmore said.

We all watched the next hit soar up again. No one spoke. The ball fell on the ground.

"How about the person *closest* to the ball calls it and the others back them up?" he tried again.

The next hit went flying to the left into the trees that lined the park. There was a yelp, a flash of falling arms and legs, and a thud.

We all rushed over. It was Miss Apfelbaum. She pulled the leaves and twigs from her hair as she struggled to stand.

"Are you all right?" Coach Blackmore took her arm to help her up.

"Oh no! You scared him away!"

Coach Blackmore looked around in alarm as if he was afraid more people were going to fall out of the trees.

"Who?" There was a definite edge of panic in his voice.

"The cerulean warbler," Miss Apfelbaum explained patiently. "He was right over there."

"Surreal what?"

"Cerulean. It's a shade of blue." She peered at him. "You're not a birder, are you?"

"No, I'm a postman."

To Miss Apfelbaum, anyone who wasn't into bird-watching was a little strange.

"Hmm. Well, they're quite rare, you know. Quite an addition to my life list." She smiled broadly.

His hand was still on her arm. He blushed deeply and pulled it back.

"Well, if the warbler is gone, I might as well go, too." Miss Apfelbaum brushed off her pants. "Nice hit, Stewy, by the way. You just need to straighten it out, my dear."

"Thanks, Miss Apfelbaum. Sorry I knocked you off your branch," Stewy said.

"No harm done." She smiled sweetly, picked up her binoculars, and walked away.

I was glad when Coach Blackmore called it a day. That

was the longest practice we had ever had. As we put the equipment away, he pulled out a stack of papers.

"Okay, gentlemen and lady," he smiled at Sophie. "Our next game is Saturday, here at Bluffton Park." He checked his clipboard. "We're playing the Alma Pirates." He looked up. "How do we normally do against the Pirates?"

"We lose," I said. Coach Blackmore had better get used to that idea right away.

"Oh, they're a pretty good team, are they?" Mr. Blackmore asked.

"Nah, we lose to everyone. We stink," said Tim.

"Not everyone," Tom argued. "I think we beat the purple team once."

"Only six of their players showed up that day," Tim reminded him. "They had to use one kid's kindergarten brother, and we lent them Dale and Sanjay."

"So basically, we beat a six-year-old and a couple of our own players?" Mr. Blackmore asked.

"Well, maybe we only tied," admitted Tom.

"Great. See you guys Saturday."

INTERCOUNTY PEEWEE
BASEBALL LEAGUE

May 22, 20-

Dear Harmony Terriers' team parents,

As the new coach of your child's baseball team, I would like to take this opportunity to pass along some information for this season.

Principal Barnes has stated that notes from coaches citing "tournament stress," "double-header exhaustion," "pop-fly neck strain," and "championship meltdown" will not be accepted as reasons to skip class tests.

Mr. Swenson has asked that I remind all ball players that cleats are not allowed in the hardware store as his wooden floors are becoming full of dimples.

Also, Mr. McCready sends his thanks to whoever hit the foul ball that struck the weathervane on his carriage house. It is working again after pointing northwest for two years.

I hope your child is looking forward to a summer of learning new skills and having fun playing a great sport. I know I am looking forward to coaching them all.

Go Terriers!

Sincerely,

Coach William Blackmore

 CHAPTER 4

Before the start of the game against the Pirates, we all huddled together for our pep talk. I waited for the usual speech about just going out and having fun and not worrying about winning. But I *was* worried about winning. I don't know why, but I kinda felt like if we started winning, our village wouldn't be this nowhere place that didn't matter.

We stood in a circle around Coach Blackmore. He just stared at us.

"Why are you all wearing different shirts?" he asked finally.

"Our sponsor had to take some of them back last year," Sophie spoke up. "Something about his ex getting half of everything. We had to dig up some hand-me-downs."

"So," Coach Blackmore seemed to be choosing his words carefully, "that's why we have two number eights?"

"Yeah," said Stewy, "only we call one *light-green* eight and one *dark-green* eight to tell them apart."

"Right."

It was plain to me it was going to take a lot more than two number eights to rattle Coach Blackmore.

"Stewy, I watched you throw at practice. I want to try you as pitcher. You have a good arm, there."

"Okay, Coach." Stewy grabbed a ball and ran onto the field.

"Scott, you seem to have a good eye on the game. Let's put you in as catcher. Clay, I want you on first base, but go help Stewy warm up until Scott gets his gear on."

I sprinted out to home plate to catch for Stewy. First base! I was excited and nervous. Excited because first base usually sees a lot of action. And nervous because, well, first base sees a lot of action. My record for catching the ball was pretty bad. I didn't want to be the one to mess up at our first game with a new coach.

Coach put Tim on second base, Sophie on third, and Tom at shortstop.

"Sanjay, Dale and Sheldon, you take the outfield. But I want you guys to back up the infield, okay?"

Dale snapped a bubble and nodded. The three fielders grabbed their gloves and headed out onto the field.

Coach stood at the opening to our dugout, did a strong double clap and called out, "Okay, team. Let's get mobile."

I felt bad for him…he seemed so optimistic.

The game went pretty much as I expected. The Pirates

mercied us the first four innings, scoring their maximum six runs each time before letting us have a turn at bat.

We actually managed a couple of hits, but our batters were left stranded on the bases and we didn't score so much as one run.

"Do you realize our team doesn't even *do* enough to bother having statistics?" Scott said, looking at the scorecard.

"Sure we do. We have a losing streak of 100%," I said, kicking the stones with my feet.

"We're only a quarter of the way through the season," Scott said. "We've still got time to turn it around."

"Way to battle, Sophie," Coach Blackmore called after she struck out.

We sat hunched on the bench. As the Pirates ran back to their dugout, number three laughed and spat in our direction.

We didn't usually react to the jokes other teams made, but I think Stewy was pretty frustrated by the game. "Bug off!" he called to him.

"Aww. Being a Terrier must be the *pits!*" number three said loud enough for all the Pirates to hear. They roared with laughter.

Coach Blackmore looked bewildered. He didn't know about the "ARM P I T" sign yet. He didn't realize that he had moved to a place where even the town's name was a joke.

"Shake it off, guys," Coach told us. "Let's shut them down at the plate."

I could barely drag myself onto the field.

"Hey, Sheldo," Stewy said as he headed to centre field. "Be ready for this first guy. He's a good hitter and most of his balls go into right field."

Sheldon was a good sport about his nickname. His aunt had misjudged the iron-on letters on one of his t-shirts so the 'n' was hidden under his arm. I wondered if he ever even told her.

"You ready?" Scott asked me, tossing me a ball. I lobbed it back to Dale on the pitching mound.

Oh, I was ready all right. Ready to be mercied again.

But then the unthinkable happened.

With only one out and the bases loaded again, the Pirates' number eleven came up to bat. Dale pitched a fastball. The batter hit a line drive past him right to Tim, who was standing on second base. The guy on second had taken a decent lead off and didn't stand a chance of getting back before Tim caught the ball with his foot planted on second. I couldn't believe my ears when I heard the umpire call the batter out on the fly and then call the runner from second out on the tag. A double play! I wasn't sure how we did it, but it was awesome anyway. All of us whooped and hollered and threw our gloves in the air.

"You guys know you're still losing, right?" The Pirates'

number six sneered at me as he ran by. I didn't care. I knew there was no way we could catch up to them even with our best at bat in history—but we had just made a double play. The first I could ever remember. We were on the way up. I could feel it.

Holmesville Gazette

Regional Sports News

Intercounty Baseball: Who's on First?

Only a few weeks into the new season for the Intercounty Peewee League and it looks like it will be an exciting year of baseball.

Last year's champions, the Sauble Sabres, have sliced through the competition so far this year. But on the weekend the Alma Pirates robbed the Sabres of a perfect record by beating them in a close game.

The Terranceville Tigers are tearing up the ball diamond with their hitting and the Barton Bulldogs are taking a bite out of their competition with a strong infield. The Dryden Hornets are putting the sting to the other teams by being the fastest around the bases.

The Harmony Terriers are good sports but seem to be chasing their tails while trying to get out of last place.

Check the league website for games and times. We hope to see you at the ballpark!

CHAPTER 5

When Scott and I showed up for practice after school, everyone was already there except for Coach Blackmore.

Stewy sat on top of the old metal climbing dome. It had definitely seen better days. The paint had peeled off most of the bars and some rust was showing in the joints. "Hey, who's up for a game of dome tag?" he called.

"We're not supposed to play that anymore, remember?" Tim said.

"Aw, come on. One chipped tooth? Your mom overreacted, Tim," Stewy said. "Besides, there's no one here to tell on us."

"What if Coach Blackmore sees us?" Sophie asked.

"He probably doesn't even know about our moms banning dome tag," Stewy scoffed. "Look, I'll even be *it*."

I couldn't resist taking him up on that challenge. You wouldn't think it, but Stewy could really move on that thing. He was hardly ever *it*.

Hats and gloves went flying as we all took our positions. Dome tag was like regular tag except you couldn't let your feet touch the ground or you were *it*. If you got tagged, you had to sit on the grass inside the dome until someone hung upside down to unfreeze you.

It was a wild game that evening, probably because we hadn't played it for so long. I guess we were screaming and laughing pretty loud because I almost didn't hear Tom. I was just hanging upside down trying to reach Sophie when he said, "Uh oh."

We froze when we realized Coach Blackmore was standing there watching us.

Everyone scrambled off the dome and grabbed their baseball stuff.

"Sorry I'm late," Coach Blackmore said, "but the bingo game went longer than I expected." His eyes went from us to the dome and back to us. "So, that wasn't the 'dome tag' game that I hear was banned, was it?"

We groaned. Now we were in for it. All he had to do was dial any one of our home phone numbers and the mom police would be all over us, waving dentist bills and grounding us for the whole summer.

I couldn't even look at him. I studied my shoes instead.

"Everyone still got all their teeth?" he asked.

I looked up at him. He was smiling. We all nodded.

"Okay, then. I'm glad I didn't see anything I'd have to report. This time." He turned and walked back to where he had dropped the equipment bag. "Hustle over, team!" he called, pulling out bats and balls. "We've got work to do."

It took a second for it to sink in that he wasn't going to rat us out. Then we galloped over to him, laughing and smiling.

Stewy punched me in the arm, "I told ya."

I was sure that was going to leave a bruise.

"Let's have everyone in the outfield and we'll practice fielding grounders." We ran onto the grass. Coach Blackmore picked up a bat and hit the balls out to us.

You'd think that a ball rolling on the ground would be easier to catch than one up in the air, but it isn't. No matter where I put my glove, that little ball found a way around it and through my legs instead.

"Remember to put your body in front of it, Clay," Coach told me. "And let's see you guys back him up out there," he called to the rest of the team. "Sheldo, if Clay is going for the ball from first base, run over from right field to grab it if he misses it. You guys are a team, remember. Help each other out."

He hit another one right at me. I got down in front of it and tried to stop it, but the ball bounced off my glove and hit my chin.

"Way to stop the ball, Clay," Coach called. "Good back up, Sheldo. *Now* you guys are getting the hang of it." He gave us the thumbs up.

Even as I rubbed my chin, I beamed at the praise. I was starting to like practice.

"Okay, everyone in," Coach Blackmore called, waving with his arm.

I started to jog back when I noticed Scott catching up to me. He wasn't jogging, he was running. I looked over my shoulder at him and he was grinning. Well, if he wanted to race, I was game. I put on a burst of speed. Scott answered by stretching those long legs of his.

The rest of the team caught on and within seconds we were pelting across the field. Everyone was running flat out as we hit the gravel of the infield.

I think I could have won if I hadn't been distracted by Stewy's war cry.

"*Ahhhhwoooo!*" he screamed as he pounded behind us. It sounded like a cross between a jumbo jet and an injured dog.

It was the most ridiculous sound I had ever heard. I couldn't help it—I started laughing. I gasped for air as Sophie passed me at the last second.

We all smashed into the backstop because there was no way we could stop when we were running that hard.

Coach Blackmore wiped the dust off his glasses. "Okay, now that we've burned off some energy, let's see how you guys are at bunting."

Bunting. Now we were talking. If there was one thing our team was good at, it was "not hitting the ball very far."

Still, even bunting gave us some trouble. Coach

Blackmore wanted us to bunt the ball about halfway down the third baseline. He said that was the hardest spot for the other team to get to fast, and from there they had to throw it the farthest to get the batter out at first.

I thought it would be easy, but whenever I tried it, the ball would just die, right there in front of home plate so that all Scott had to do was pick it up and tag me. I hadn't even left home plate and I was out.

The others didn't have much better luck, even though Coach tried to show us the right way to hold the bat, turn our bodies and aim the ball down and to the left. Hard to believe, but I guess we weren't that great at *not* hitting the ball, either.

I hoped I never had to bunt in a game. It would be a disaster.

After practice, Coach Blackmore passed around a white cardboard box full of pastry for us.

"Awesome danish," Stewy told him.

For some reason, that made Coach Blackmore blush.

Harmony Point Post Office

From: Mark Hartley [m.hartley@canadapost.gc.ca]

To: William Blackmore [harmony.point@canadapost.gc.ca]

CC: Andrew Jones

Subject: Efficiency review at Harmony Point Post Office

Dear Mr. Blackmore,

Just wanted to let you know that someone from the accounting department will drop in on you this week. Could you please dig out all your records for him, including expense sheets and invoices? We want to have a look at your numbers.

Thanks,

Mark Hartley
Head Office
Canada Post

CHAPTER 6

"So, what are our chances?" I asked Scott in the middle of our game of War on Monday after school.

"Chances of what?" he asked, taking my queen with an ace.

"Of winning a game," I said. "It's only been a few weeks with Mr. Blackmore as our coach, but we already catch more balls than we drop. And we even scored a few runs at our last game. I think there just might have been a few minutes during the last game when the Wolves weren't laughing at us. It's only a matter of time till we win, right?"

Scott squinted like he was going to work out some equation in his head when I heard someone coming.

As soon as we saw it was Stewy lumbering full speed up my front walk, gasping for breath, we knew it had to be serious. Stewy doesn't lumber unless he *really* has to.

"What's wrong, Stewy?" I called. "Are you having a heart attack or something?"

He stopped at the bottom of the steps, trying to catch his breath.

Scott and I left our card game and ran to his side. Stewy took a couple of minutes to answer. He was rasping and wheezing, and his face was bright red.

"No. It's not, *huh*, me. It's, *huh*, Coach, *huh*, Blackmore."

"What is? *What* is Coach Blackmore?" I asked, willing him to breathe. Whatever the news was, it had to be bad. Stewy couldn't even answer.

"A stroke? Car accident? Rabies?" Scott asked, his eyes wide.

"How could he have rabies?" I scoffed.

"There are over 2,000 cases of rabies in humans each year," Scott said, defensively.

Where did he get this stuff?

"Is it rabies, Stewy?" I asked.

Stewy shook his head *no*.

"He's leaving," he finally wheezed.

"Leaving?" I repeated. "He can't be leaving. He just got here!"

"He hasn't even called the second bingo game yet," Scott added.

Stewy shook his head again. "A man from Canada Post came into the post office this morning when I was getting the mail. I heard him say something about how they were re-thinking the need for a post office here. Everything will be moved to the city."

We were stunned into silence.

"They can't be serious," I said finally. "We've had a post office in that building forever. My dad told me Old Pearl ran it for something like forty years before Mrs. Stanfield's father came. And he was there for ages until he finally retired and she took over. That's gotta be about a hundred years! It's part of our history. They *can't* close it down."

"It sure looks like they can," Stewy said, having got his breath back. "He said he was coming back in a couple of months to see the final numbers."

"What numbers?" Scott asked.

"The number of letters coming through, I guess. Maybe they don't think there's enough mail to keep it open."

"This is crazy," I said. "Just when you think there is nothing left to lose, someone thinks of something else to take."

"No post office?" Scott said. "No more town news? No more mail?"

"Forget the mail. How about no more baseball coach?" I said.

"Geez," said Stewy. "And just when we were getting good, too."

The three of us stood in moody silence staring at the ground. So much for turning the team around. So much for winning for Harmony Point.

I couldn't let it happen. I couldn't stand to lose even one more thing.

I lifted my head. "Call an emergency team meeting. Bluffton Park. Thirty minutes."

WELCOME TO
BLUFFTON PARK!

Home of the
World Thumb War Championships

This land donated by
Fred McCready and family
to commemorate the great turnip harvest of
1943.

Please keep all pets on a leash.
Stoop and scoop laws are in effect.

CHAPTER 7

The Grim Reaper would have looked positively cheerful compared to the ten faces that stared back at me from the park bleachers when I told them the news.

"Do you think it's all a big mistake?" Tim said. "Maybe that Canada Post guy got us mixed up with another town?"

"Numbers don't lie, Tim," Scott said.

"But why does Coach Blackmore have to leave?" Sophie asked. "Couldn't he just get another job in Harmony?"

"Doing what? Half our parents had to find work in the city already," Tom said. "Besides, he's probably under contract with the post office. They'll just move him."

"So they'll move him to the city. What's the big deal?" Sophie said. "He can commute from there and still be our coach."

"I don't think so," I said. "I heard my mom tell Sanjay's mom that he'd applied to the city in the first place, but there weren't any openings. Who knows where they'll send him?"

"Oh," she said. "Well, would your dad coach us, Stewy? He's into sports, isn't he?"

"My dad's idea of a sport is seeing how many submarine

sandwiches he can make during halftime of a football game."

"Well, I guess we can beg Mr. Meyers to coach us again," Sophie said with a sigh.

The others nodded.

I looked from face to face. What was wrong with them? Didn't they know what was at stake here? Didn't they understand that we were on the verge of losing everything?

"That's it?" I said. "You're all okay with Coach Blackmore leaving? You're not going to do anything?"

"What do you want us to do, Clay? You know what they say," said Tom. "You can't fight Canada Post."

"I thought the saying was 'You can't fight City Hall'?" Sophie asked.

"Yeah, well we don't *have* a City Hall anymore, remember?" Tom said, gloomily.

It was like they had given up already. Well, I wasn't about to sit back and just let some big shots come in and wipe out our post office, not to mention our baseball team.

"Coach Blackmore is the first real coach we've ever had," I said. "We actually made a double play at the last game. We were hitting. We were catching. It felt *good*, didn't it?" I looked from one kid to another. "Didn't it?"

"Yeah, it felt good," Stewy admitted. "So what is it you want us to do?"

What *did* I want them to do? It's not like we could

47

phone up Canada Post and demand they keep our post office open. Nobody listens to a bunch of kids. We were going to have to play it their way.

"We're going to get the mail moving," I said. "Like Scott said, numbers don't lie. If we get enough mail flowing through Harmony, they won't close it down and we won't lose our coach."

"Now, how are we supposed to do that?" Tim asked.

A plan started to form in my head. A pretty good plan, I thought. "We're going to write letters. Lots of them. There's going to be a paper blizzard at the Post Office. Coach Blackmore will need hip waders to get to the counter."

"Won't work," Sophie said.

"Why not?" I asked.

"Because they don't count *outgoing* mail; they count *incoming* mail. Outgoing mail only needs a mailbox. People need to write to *us*."

Rats. A glitch in my pretty good plan.

"So, we ask questions then," I said. "That way they have to answer. Or ask for things."

"Wait. I don't know anybody to write to," Tim said. "Besides, won't it look suspicious if all the letters are addressed to us?"

"He's right," Tom said. "Maybe we should use fake names."

48

"That's no good, either," Sophie said. "If it's not a real address, then the mail won't be delivered." She wasn't going to make this easy, was she?

"But we *could* use the addresses of other people in Harmony," I said, not willing to give up. "Kinda write letters *for* them."

"That's a great idea," Stewy said, grinning. "I think the Carters behind our house with the five kids would love some brochures on summer camps. All those kids do all summer is scream."

Sophie shook her head. "You can't do that. You can't write letters pretending to be someone else. That's called misrepresentation, and it's against the law."

Now she was really starting to bug me.

Scott spoke up. "So what *can* we do that won't get us arrested?"

"Well, we can still write letters on their behalf," Sophie said. "We just can't pretend to *be* them."

"I don't get it," Stewy said.

"Write to a camp and say you know a family that would be interested in sending their five screaming kids away for the summer and could they send them some information," Sophie suggested.

"A summer without those lunatics is definitely worth a letter," Stewy said. "I'm going to get it in the mail today!"

Everyone was talking and laughing as we jumped down from the bleachers. I had a good feeling about this. Harmony Point wasn't going to lose this time.

St. Ursula's

Join us every Thursday evening
for fun and prizes!

St. Ursula's Hall
(please use the entrance off the parking lot
and watch your head on the low doorway!)

Games start: 5:00 PM

Special JACKPOT game
Full house wins you your choice of:

Free oil changes for a year
(Courtesy of Joe's Auto)
Or
Five cords of hardwood
(Courtesy of Harlan Moore)
Or
One free taxidermy (raccoon or smaller)
(Courtesy of Byers Taxidermy and Framing)

CHAPTER 8

"Clay! It's right above you!"

Having Stewy scream at me didn't help me locate the ball in the glare of the overhead lights.

Clunk.

I could finally see the ball. It was on the ground by my feet. Another run for the Sabers. We were already losing badly and it was only the second inning.

I didn't like night games. On Wednesdays, our games didn't start until seven in the evening and that meant I had to do my homework right after school instead of catching my favourite shows. And even though the days were getting longer, it still ended up being dark before the game was over. It also meant that for the last part of the game, we had to play under the lights. It wasn't so bad at some of the other teams' fields. They had lights that didn't blind you every time you tried to catch a fly ball.

But Bluffton Park's lights teetered on old wooden poles and were positioned so that looking up was like looking at the sun without sunglasses. For several minutes afterwards, I had spots in front of my eyes and couldn't have seen a giant meteor, let alone a baseball.

"Shake it off, Clay," Coach Blackmore called.

Sure. Shake it off. It's pretty hard to do that when the guy is standing beside you, snickering under his breath.

We lost a couple more pop flies in the lights and the inning was finally over. I could only hope that the Sabers would have as much trouble with the lights as we did. Of course, that would mean we would have to hit the ball.

"Okay, Scott, you're up. Protect the plate, buddy," Coach Blackmore said.

Scott managed a weak grounder. The ball was easy to spot as it drifted along the grass and he was thrown out at first.

Tom struck out. Didn't look like the lights were going to be any problem for the Sabers.

"Show us how it's done, Sophie," Coach called.

She grabbed a bat leaning against the backstop and swung it around.

"Get a load of this," the Saber on third called. "They're sending in a *girl!*" The other Sabers laughed.

"Hey, this is a diamond, but I don't think it's the kind you were looking for!" the second baseman yelled. That got him an even bigger laugh.

I wished I could say something smart back at those guys, but I couldn't think of anything.

"Don't let them get to you, Soph," was all I could say.

Sophie looked at me and smiled. "They don't bother me," she said, a little glint in her eye.

I smiled back. I knew that look. She was going to let her bat do the talking.

The first pitch came in right at her knees.

"Strike!"

The Sabers were all smiles.

The pitcher went into his wind-up for the second pitch.

There was a loud crack as her bat made contact with the ball. She took off like a bullet from home plate. Her lanky legs were a blur as she headed for first base. The outfielder was still chasing the ball, so Sophie rounded first and headed for second. We were cheering like mad.

The outfielder made a grab for the ball, twisted his body, and threw to second. The second baseman caught it and got ready to tag her.

Sophie skidded to a stop two-thirds of the way there. She whirled and headed back to first. The loudmouth on second threw to first. The first baseman caught the ball and got ready to tag her. She stopped.

Sophie was trapped in a rundown.

In a battle of speed and wits, I'd put my money on Sophie every time, but these guys were slowly closing in on her. Back and forth they threw the ball as she headed toward first and then back to second and then back to first.

They were getting closer and closer, but Sophie never lost her cool. She was so quick in changing direction that their throws started to get more frantic. The second baseman was getting frustrated and he fumbled a bad throw from first. The ball went skidding past second base and he had to scramble to pick it up. It was all Sophie needed.

She took off like she had wings on her cleats. About two strides before the base she dropped and slid. It was like watching a slow-motion movie as we saw her foot make contact with the base a fraction of a second before the second baseman swiped her ankle with his glove.

"Safe!"

I couldn't hear what the guy on second said to her, but it made Sophie grin. He stood over her with the ball ready to tag her if she so much as moved an inch off the bag while trying to get up.

"Time, ump?" Sophie asked, making a T with her two hands.

The umpire put both arms up. "Time!" he called.

Sophie could get up without getting tagged now. She casually brushed the dust off her pants, moved to the other side of the base, and got ready to run. The guy just glared at her. She grinned.

Stewy came up to the plate. The pitcher stood ready. Sophie moved away from the bag. He looked over his shoulder and then fired to second, but Sophie was ready for him. She sprinted back.

"Safe!"

I was barely breathing. Stewy had a good chance of hitting her home, but not if Sophie got thrown out at second. I kinda wished she would hang closer to the base because these guys looked like they were out to get her.

The pitcher held the ball and looked over his right shoulder again. Sophie moved a few steps away from second, staying in her crouch position, arms outstretched, ready to go one way or the other.

The pitcher fired to second again. Sophie bolted towards the base, but the second baseman was so busy watching her out of the corner of his eye that he missed the ball.

There was a cloud of dust as Sophie skidded, whirled, and took off for third. We were almost hoarse from screaming. The centre fielder ran forward to grab the ball and tossed it to third. It was a wild throw that was nowhere near his man, and it sailed out of bounds.

"Time!" the base umpire called.

Sophie, about to round third, came to a stop. She didn't even look winded.

"Out of play. You," the umpire said pointing at Sophie. "Go to home."

The guy on second threw his glove to the ground and kicked at it.

Sophie jogged to home plate and did a little leap to land on it with both feet. The rest of our team was lined up just past home plate to give Sophie high fives. Even Coach Blackmore.

We ended up losing nine to one, but we didn't mind. That one run was the most fun we'd had at a game in a long time.

June 8, 20-

Mrs. Pamela Morelli
74 Parson's Lane
Harmony Point, ON
N1S 7C5

Dear Mrs. Morelli,

We were very glad to hear from one of your students, Sanjay Patel, that you are interested in having your class participate in our Sea-Chimps in Space program next September. The packets of Sea-Chimp eggs you will receive in the fall were carried aboard the International Space Station for one year. We are interested in studying the effects of zero gravity on the growth of these exciting creatures.

As your class watches their sea creatures grow, we hope you will notify us of any unusual findings. We are especially interested in Sea-Chimps with extra tails or heads, or creatures that swim backwards, upside down, or not at all.

PLEASE NOTE: In the unlikely event that you notice the growth of excessively large teeth or cannibalism among your Sea-Chimps, please call our Emergency Hotline number immediately. Do not put fingers or other body parts in the tank without protection.

Enjoy growing these adorable sea creatures!

John Bertram

John Bertram
President
Sea-Chimps R Us

Our next game against the Bulldogs wasn't worth remembering. Even though we had come a long way with our skills thanks to Coach's drills, we still didn't seem to be able to show our stuff at the games. I didn't want to admit that the other teams intimidated us, but they did.

The field was still damp from a summer shower and the bits of grass from the last mowing stuck to our sneakers as Scott and I walked to the bleachers where the rest of the team was waiting for Coach before the start of practice.

"So?" Sophie asked, when we got close.

"So, what?" I said.

"The letter-writing campaign—that's what. How is it going?"

"Oh, pretty good. I've sent out four already," Scott answered. "I'm even trying to get us a sponsor for our team."

"I'm working on Regional Council," I said. "I'm asking them for all kinds of things, starting with getting our town sign fixed. Man! I hate looking at that thing. What about the rest of you?"

"I sent away for a whole bunch of free offers at the

back of my subscription to Kids' Science magazine," Sanjay added. "Maybe Mrs. Morelli will have something other than a bunch of bean sprouts on the windowsill for us to observe next year."

"I got the camp letter done," Stewy said. "It was pretty good, too, if I do say so myself."

"That's it, Stewy? *One* letter?" I asked.

Stewy looked offended. "Hey! It took me all day to write that!"

"What Clay means," Sophie said, "is that it takes time for people to write back and you said Mr. Canada Post was coming back in a couple of months. We've got to step it up if we're going to see any results."

"Oh yeah? Well, how many have *you* written?" Stewy asked her, his arms folded.

"Fourteen. And I have ideas for three more for tonight."

Stewy's mouth hung open.

I was glad Coach Blackmore showed up for practice just then. I didn't want to admit to Sophie that I'd only written three letters so far.

Coach had us start with our throwing drill. This time, Scott and I made it back seven steps before I missed the ball. It was a new record for us. In fact, we were all getting better at throwing and catching.

"You guys are really getting the hang of this," Coach said, looking at his clipboard for Wednesday's game information. "Let's see some of these strong arms at our game against the Tigers."

Coach Blackmore did his best to pump us up before the game on Saturday, but the minute we took the field, our confidence went down the drain. Again.

The other teams in their matching jerseys and caps always looked so *together*—so sure of themselves. We weren't sure of anything.

The Tigers pulverized us the first three innings. I forget how many runs they got. Let's just say it was a lot.

We had some good hitters now, especially since Coach Blackmore had been working on our technique, but every time one of us went up to bat we seemed to just lose our nerve or something.

The Tigers' pitcher was this tall skinny kid who had a wicked fastball and a nasty reputation. More than one team's coach had complained to the league about the number of times he hit someone with the ball. Sure, if he nailed you, you were awarded an automatic walk to first… but that's if you still *could* walk.

The fourth inning started off like the rest. Stewy managed to hit one of that kid's wild pitches, but he got thrown out at first. Then Tim struck out. Scott was next up to bat.

The first pitch came right for Scott's chest. He jumped out of the way just in time.

"Ball one."

Scott's back was tense and his mouth tight. The pitcher went into his wind-up. The ball came screaming at Scott's head. He turned to get out of the way, but the ball made contact. He went down like a stone and didn't move. Coach Blackmore went running out but told us to stay put. We crammed up against the backstop to try and get a look. Coach bent down and spoke to Scott. I could see Scott move and put his hand to his face.

Instead of looking like he was sorry, the pitcher was grinning. The other players on his team were joking that the pitcher was going to get another mark on his helmet.

I couldn't believe it. These guys thought it was funny that Scott was hurt.

Coach Blackmore helped Scott get up and walk to the bench. Scott said he was fine and that his helmet took most of the hit. But the ball must have got him a bit because his left eye was swelling up pretty good.

"Who was last out?" Coach asked, getting an ice pack out of his first-aid kit.

"I was," said Tim.

"Go and take Scott's place on first. Who's up to bat?"

"I am," I said. My blood was pounding through my veins with anger. I grabbed a bat and went to the plate while Tim jogged to first.

For the first time I wasn't afraid of the ball. I wanted a piece of that guy. I hoped I hit it right at his head. No one, I mean *no one*, hits my best friend and gets away with it.

The first pitch was a bit low but I swung anyway. The ball went skidding down through the gap between second and third. I ran flat out to first and could hear everyone on our bench cheering for me. Tim looked back at me from second base and gave me a nod. Sophie was up next. I couldn't see her eyes, but by the way she walked up to the plate I knew she meant business, too.

A beautiful line drive brought both Tim and me home. Sophie was stranded on second as the Sheldo struck out, but we had two runs in. As the three of us jogged back to our bench, I was still pretty pumped up from being so mad. I could see Sophie and Tim felt the same way. Scott gave us the thumbs up from behind his ice pack.

Tom took over as catcher and with some solid pitching by Stewy, we kept the Tigers to one run.

By the end of the game, we were like a new team. Sure, we still lost—but we had a whole new attitude.

June 11, 20-

Mr. & Mrs. Bob Carter
8 Old Pine Line
Harmony Point, ON
N1S 1B3

Dear Mr. and Mrs. Carter:

I understand that you are interested in the summer camp experience for your family. Thank you for considering Camp Wannasendemtous. We offer varied and flexible programs designed to accommodate children of all ages and abilities. I have included this year's brochure and you will notice we offer discounts to families with more than one child attending.

While we are proud of our innovative and current therapeutic programs for children with special needs, I must admit we have never considered using scream therapy. I am happy to report, though, that our grounds are extensive and our neighbours quite distant, so your children's natural exuberance should not be a problem.

Our campers are able to learn new skills through activities such as archery, kayaking and rock climbing. While these are not designed specifically to wear our campers out, we do find an active lifestyle contributes to healthy sleeping habits.

If you are planning on applying, please be sure to leave us at least three emergency contact numbers.

Sincerely,

Stewart Parsons

Stewart Parsons
Camp Director

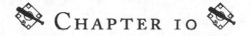

Coach Blackmore met us Saturday afternoon at the Dryden ballpark for our next game. It had a covered grandstand, loudspeakers, and an electronic scoreboard. It felt like we were playing in the major leagues.

Coach had us do some laps around the field and stretches to warm up. He told us that our pre-game routine was the same one the Blue Jays used. You know, it made us feel like a real team.

"I heard Mrs. Carter tell my mom yesterday that they were going to send their kids to camp this year, Stewy," I said, doing a lunge to pull my leg muscles.

Stewy stopped stretching and lay back on the grass, his arms behind his head and a look of bliss on his face. "Ahhh, I can hear the crickets already."

"Do you think our plan is working yet?" Tim asked. "'Cuz I'm running out of money for stamps."

We all looked at Scott. "Well, given the rate of return, times the number of letters each of us has written, I'd say the mail should be pouring in," he said.

That was good news.

Coach Blackmore called us to the dugout.

The Dryden Hornets took the field. The game started out pretty well; after a couple of innings we had scored two runs on some bad throws by the Hornets' infield and were only trailing by two points. I was sure this was where we would turn our luck around.

"Go, Terriers, go!" It was Miss Apfelbaum sitting among some of the parents. Was it my imagination or was she showing up at a lot of the games all of a sudden?

We held our own for the beginning of the game, but by the third inning we were slipping. By the fourth, we were down by eight runs and it was getting hard to keep positive. Stewy's pitching had started out strong but now the ball was swooping and diving like a seagull in a windstorm. I got that same old sinking feeling.

"Way to mix them up, Stewy," Coach Blackmore called as if Stewy had thrown the ball into the Hornets' dugout on purpose.

Stewy shook his head and kicked at the pitcher's mound.

The next Hornets batter took a few practice swings. Scott squatted down behind home plate and signalled the pitch to Stewy. Stewy shook his head. Scott signalled again. Stewy shook his head again. Scott called a time out and I went with him out to the mound to see what was going on with Stewy.

"Why you keep shaking your head, Stew?" Scott asked him under his breath.

"'Cuz I haven't got the least idea what pitch you're signalling when you move your whole hand around in circles like that."

"That's not part of the signal. I've just got a cramp in my wrist from too much typing."

"Yeah, I know how you feel. I think I've got tennis elbow. All those letters are killing me!"

Why did I get the feeling this was going to be blamed on me?

"Just throw the ball where he can catch it, okay?" I told Stewy, "Otherwise that guy on third is going to steal home." They already had three runs this inning and I sure didn't want to be mercied again.

"I'll try," Stewy said. We jogged back to our bases.

"Okay, Stewy. Like you can," Coach Blackmore called and clapped his hands twice.

The pitch went wild. It bounced right out of Scott's glove and started rolling down toward first base. Stewy, Scott, and I all ran flat out for it. We smacked into each other just as we reached the ball. Jeers came from the other bench. Three more runs for the Hornets. Mercied again. Game over.

"Good hustle, team!" Coach Blackmore clapped his hands like we had just made a great play instead of looking like characters in a cartoon. "Way to chase down that ball. How about we just let the one person get it next time, okay?"

His only answer was some grumbles and gloves thrown at the bench.

Coach Blackmore went to help Scott get his catcher equipment off.

"Hey, Clay. Have you asked Coach Blackmore about the mail?" Stewy asked quietly, rubbing his elbow. "Is there a paper avalanche yet?"

"I don't know. I tried to talk to him after Mr. Jackson's funeral, but everyone was pretty shook up about what happened."

"Why? What happened?" Tim asked.

"I guess the hearse hit a pretty big pothole and the coffin went flying. My dad said they're lucky they had closed the lid tight or Mr. Jackson might have been sitting in the driver's seat."

"You know, they should do something about that road," Tom said. "Maybe someone should write to the town council and remind them." He winked.

"Anyway, I didn't get a chance to ask Coach about the mail," I said.

"Well, ask soon. After this game, I could use some good news," Stewy said.

I knew how he felt.

June 16, 20-

Councillor Gary Wilson
Holmesville Town Council
Harmony Point, ON
N1S 7C4

Dear Mr. Wilson,

A concerned citizen in your district has asked me to contact you in reference to the state of the roads in the area and our mandate to fix them.

Please let me reassure you that we have not forgotten that Highway 51 is our responsibility. It was only an oversight that the repairs we had slated for this summer got bumped by expansion of the Redhaven Expressway.

I am sure that no one on Regional Council finds it funny that a casket nearly bounced off the back of a hearse because of the potholes, and we would all like to offer our condolences to the family of the deceased.

The resurfacing and repainting project should be able to start within the next two months.

Sincerely,

Jack Bridgeman

Jack Bridgeman
Works Department
Municipality of Dundurn

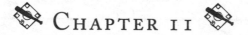

CHAPTER 11

On the way home from school on Tuesday, I detoured to the post office. I stood in line and watched Miss Apfelbaum search through her purse for change. Mr. Blackmore waited for her to count out enough for one stamp.

"We sell books of stamps, too," he said, trying to be helpful.

Didn't he know that a book of stamps would defeat the purpose of Miss Apfelbaum's almost daily visits? I mean, her cheeks blushed pink every time their hands touched. The endless boxes of danish at practices were no longer a mystery.

Miss Apfelbaum handed her letter to Mr. Blackmore so that he could attach the stamp.

"No stamp necessary for this one, Miss Apfelbaum." He handed it back to her.

"Call me Myra," she said breathlessly.

"P..p...please call me William," he stuttered.

I couldn't help it. I rolled my eyes.

After Miss Apfelbaum floated out the door, I went up to the counter, curious.

"Why didn't Miss Apfelbaum's letter need a stamp?" I asked.

"Letters to Members of Parliament don't need a stamp."

"Really? Why?"

"The idea is that everyone should be heard by their government regardless of whether or not they can afford postage."

Free letters. Now *that* was something I could get excited about. I mean, I know we had a worthy cause and all, but I had already used up all my savings and even an advance on next week's allowance. "Cool."

"You here for more stamps already?" Mr. Blackmore asked.

"Yeah." Was he getting suspicious? "So, how's business?" I didn't dare go back to Stewy without some news about how our plan was working so far. He had taken to rubbing his elbow every time he saw me now.

"Business?" Mr. Blackmore looked puzzled.

"Yeah, you know. You got lots of mail coming through?" I tried hard to sound casual.

"Well, it's steady." Mr. Blackmore said.

"You haven't noticed a big increase?"

"No. Should I have?"

"Uh, no. Yes. I don't know. I was just wondering." I ran out the door, my head starting to ache. I wasn't looking forward to telling this to the guys.

I was right. They were crushed.

"All those letters and he didn't even notice?" Stewy said.

"He said the mail was steady. That's an improvement," I said, trying to stay positive.

"Steady? Tennis elbow is too high a price for *steady*," Stewy said. "I figured he would be drowning in all that mail."

"If he doesn't see a difference, neither will Mr. Canada Post," Sophie said.

"It's not like this is going to work anyway," Tim said gloomily. "A bunch of kids aren't going to change anyone's mind about anything."

I didn't like where this was going.

"You guys aren't giving up, are you?" I looked from one to another. "I found out a way to mail letters without stamps," I added, hoping *that* might convince them.

"It's no use, Clay," Stewy said. "You need to learn to accept things. The post office is going to close. Coach Blackmore is going to leave. End of story."

He obviously didn't know how stubborn I could be.

"Well, I'm not going to accept that. I'm going to keep on writing letters until my fingers fall off," I said.

"Suit yourself," Stewy said. "I've got a project to finish for science class." With that he hopped off the climber and left.

Tim and Tom looked embarrassed but jumped down too. Sophie put a hand on my shoulder. "Sorry, Clay. But

Tim's right. A bunch of kids can't change anyone's mind."

I turned to Scott. "What about you?"

Scott looked at the ground. "You want to know the odds of this working out?"

I shook my head. "No numbers."

Scott sighed. "Well, yeah, I guess I'm still in. But Stewy's right, you know. You gotta learn to accept things."

We walked home in silence.

"How do you spell 'extravaganza'?" Scott asked me just as we got to his house.

"I don't know, why?"

"Well, we gotta have some reason to write to Barry Manilow," Scott said. "How about inviting him to a Bingo Extravaganza for the orphans of Harmony?"

"We don't have any orphans!" I said.

"Statistically speaking, about five percent of any population are orphans. I'm sure we could round some up if we needed to."

"You know, you scare me sometimes. And why would you want to write to Barry Manilow, anyway?"

"I think it's time he heard about his biggest fan," Scott said, grinning. "I wonder what Miss Apfelbaum will do when she gets a letter from her idol?"

"Probably faint," I said.

"And then bake him a danish," Scott added, laughing.

It took only a week for the reply to come. Scott and I were picking up the mail after school when we saw Coach Blackmore hand Miss Apfelbaum a big manila envelope. Her face turned pink as she read the return address, and she tore it open with shaking fingers. As she read the letter, her eyes opened wide and then the colour drained from her face. There was a loud thud. Miss Apfelbaum was on the floor, out cold, a signed photo of Barry Manilow clutched in her hand.

June 28, 20-

Miss Myra Apfelbaum
13 Oakridge Drive
Harmony, ON
N1S 5D3

Dear Miss Apfelbaum,

It is with great regret that I must inform you that Mr. Barry Manilow will not be able to commit to appearing at St. Ursula's Charity Bingo Extravaganza. While Mr. Manilow feels deeply for the plight of St. Ursula's orphans, his schedule does not permit him to attend.

Thank you for your continued support. Mr. Manilow is very grateful to his loyal fans and hopes you will accept this autographed picture as a token of his appreciation.

Sincerely,

Peter Collins

Peter Collins
Assistant to Mr. Manilow

CHAPTER 12

It was obvious something was wrong with the team. Even Coach Blackmore noticed.

The practice was too quiet. No one joked or teased. Tim and Tom didn't argue. Every one of us had a long face.

I tried hard not to be sore at the team, but they had let me down. No, they had let Coach Blackmore down. If they weren't willing to stand up for Harmony Point, then maybe it really was a nowhere place with a bunch of losers.

I wished I had never written that letter to the Bricker Computer Corporation asking them to sponsor us. Some team players we were. The Terriers wouldn't even fight to keep our coach.

Coach Blackmore double-clapped, "Let's get down to business, guys and, er, gal."

We started with our throwing and catching drills. I was paired with Stewy. We just glared at each other.

"Could you at least aim the ball at my glove?" I said after the third time I had to chase a ball from a wild throw. I knew he was doing it on purpose.

"Whatever," Stewy said.

"You could at least try!" I stormed.

"I did."

"Not much."

Stewy understood right away that we weren't talking about baseball anymore.

"I did try. But I'm smart enough to know when to stop wasting my energy."

"*Quit*, you mean."

Stewy went red in the face and was about to answer but he got cut off by Coach Blackmore calling us over to the pitcher's mound.

Oh, this wasn't over by a long shot.

"Okay, guys," Coach Blackmore said looking a little worried, "Where's all that energy you usually have? Why don't we liven things up with some friendly competition?"

No one answered.

"Everyone out to the outfield. I'm going to hit pop flies and whoever is closest should call the ball. If you don't call it or you drop it, you're out. The player who is left will get a special prize."

On a normal day, the mere mention of a prize—any prize—would have us running into the field like a pack of wild dogs, but today we could barely drag our feet out onto the field.

Coach Blackmore hit the first pop fly and it headed straight for Stewy. No way was I going to let Stewy get the prize.

I rushed over calling, "I got it," and sorta shoved Stewy aside to catch it.

"Hey," Stewy pushed me back. "Watch it!"

"Oh, I'm sorry," I said—a little sarcastically, I guess. "Should I have *quit trying* to catch it?" Okay, a lot sarcastically.

Stewy stared at me. *Game on*, said the look on his face.

The next hit veered toward right field where I was standing. Stewy came charging like a rhino. "I got it!" he yelled just before plowing into me, knocking me to the ground.

"Let's watch where we're running, guys," called Coach Blackmore, his eyebrows knitted in concern.

I got up slowly, never taking my eyes off of Stewy. The rest of the team came over and stood around us.

"You're a sore loser," Stewy sneered.

"Yeah, well you're all a bunch of quitters." I knew the moment the words left my lips that the smouldering spark of anger in the team would catch fire. But you know, I didn't care.

"You just want to be a big hero, Clay," Tom said. "You know you're wasting your time."

"At least he's doing something," said Scott, coming to my defense. It was good to know I could count on one person.

"What's going on over there?" Coach Blackmore called over to us. "You're not ready to quit already, are you?"

Coach Blackmore could not have imagined the effect the word 'quit' would have on us.

The next hit was a free-for-all. "I got it," screamed ten voices as the entire group charged after the ball. It was headed straight for the trees at the edge of the field. Tom was the first to dive for it, but Scott checked him from behind and the ball flew out of his glove into the trees. Sophie got it next, but Tim grabbed it from her hand. I snatched it from Tim, but couldn't hang onto it as Stewy smacked into me. The ball flew over the bushes and landed in Bluffton Creek.

All ten of us stormed into the water. Arms and legs were flying everywhere as we all tried to grab the ball. Dale got the bright idea to take off his hat and use it to scoop water and throw it in the nearest face and soon there was water flying everywhere. I don't even know where the ball went.

I got my hat full of water and aimed for Stewy, but Stewy bent down just then to fill his own hat, and the water hit Sophie full in the face. She lost her balance and fell into the creek.

I tried to say sorry and give her a hand up, but when she took my arm she yanked me down face first into the water. She has a pretty good grip for a girl.

Stewy roared with laughter. I grabbed his ankle and pulled him down next. Soon, no leg was safe. The team fell like bowling pins. We were splashing and rolling and laughing so hard we forgot the argument. You can't laugh and be mad at the same time, you know.

Everyone went quiet when we saw Coach Blackmore standing on the bank, his arms folded.

All soggy ten of us slowly staggered to our feet and climbed out of the water. Sophie's ponytail was plastered down her back, Tim and Tom's curls were limp, and ten pairs of sneakers squished.

"Feel better now?" he asked us, trying to look stern. We looked at one another. "Maybe you two guys have something to say to each other?" he said to Stewy and me.

I guess I should've made the first move but Stewy beat me to it. He never could keep a grudge. He offered me his hand, "No hard feelings?"

What could I do but take his hand? We'd been friends since kindergarten. "Nah. No hard feelings."

"So, are we still a team?" Coach Blackmore asked.

Me and Stewy looked embarrassed. "Yeah," we both said.

"Good," Coach Blackmore said. "Because I have something for all of you."

He walked back over to his equipment bag and pulled out a large package. We gathered around while he pulled out a letter.

"It seems someone on the team thought we could

use a sponsor." Coach Blackmore gave me a long look. I squirmed a little. I hoped he wasn't mad at me for not asking him first.

Coach Blackmore reached into the package and pulled out a stack of new green jerseys. Each one had a picture of a snarling dog under the words Harmony Terriers on the front and the BCC logo over our numbers on the back. None of the shirts had holes or frayed collars. And there was only one number eight.

June 22, 20-

Mr. William Blackmore
15 Parson's Lane
Harmony, ON
N1S 8C5

**BRICKER COMPUTER
CORPORATION**

Dear Mr. Blackmore,

You seem to have an enthusiastic and ambitious team in the
Terriers. So, it is with regret that I must inform you that Bricker
Computer Corporation cannot sponsor the Harmony Terriers' trip
to play in the Player's Choice Baseball Tournament in Oshawa,
Ontario. While Bricker Computer Corp. avidly supports amateur
sports, we already have a full complement of sponsorship
commitments for this year.

We did notice, however, in the team photo you sent us that the
Terriers are lacking in some basic equipment. I am happy to tell
you that we have arranged with a supplier to provide the Terriers
with new baseball jerseys at our expense.

Bricker Computer Corporation wishes you and your team the
best of luck in your endeavours.

Go Terriers!!

Sincerely,

Brian Marsdale

Brian Marsdale
CEO
Bricker Computer Corporation

# Chapter 13

I was determined to hold the runner at first. It was hard to believe, but we were leading four to three. And at the Sabers' home park in Rossneath, too. I couldn't remember the last time we were leading in a game.

The Sabers' main pitcher was out with a sprained ankle and their substitute was a little nervous and was pitching too low. Because he walked us so many times, we got four runs in and, as Stewy would say, "a run is a run even if it's a walk." We only needed three more outs and the game would be over.

With one foot on first base, I held my glove open in front of me, ready in case Stewy decided to pivot and fire the ball.

Tagging a guy out on first was something we had been practicing with Coach Blackmore for three weeks now. We had never even tried it in a game before. Too many times, the guy on first—which was usually me—would miss the ball and the runner would steal a base or two.

The runner swaggered a long distance from the bag. He looked pretty smug about his lead-off too because everyone knew that the Terriers never picked off a runner: we never even tried.

I watched Stewy, waiting for the twitch in his left shoulder that signaled his intent to whirl and throw. Part of me wanted Stewy to pitch it at me so I could knock that smug look off the runner's face, and part of me was terrified that I would drop the ball.

The runner took another couple of steps. *Too far!* I thought. Stewy's shoulder twitched. A second later, he turned and fired the ball at me. I resisted the urge to look at the runner and kept my eye on the ball, just like Coach had taught me.

The ball smacked into my glove. I dropped my arm and brushed the runner's foot with my glove.

"Out!" the base umpire called. That was the sweetest word I ever heard an umpire say.

The runner looked at me with stunned disbelief. He got up and stood by the base, his brain unable to grasp the fact that he was really out.

"Come on, number six, HUSTLE IN," yelled the Sabers' coach, who was chewing his gum so violently I was sure he was going to dislocate his jaw.

Coach Blackmore did his double-clap thing and gave the thumbs up to Stewy and me.

There was still a runner on second. The next batter stood at home plate, flexing his knees and waving his bat over his shoulder. Stewy lifted his arms in ready position. He looked over his right shoulder at Tim on second and saw him ready with his glove. The Sabers' runner was hanging a little closer to the base than usual, clearly spooked. Stewy looked over his left shoulder at me and I saw the slight smile on his lips.

Stewy fixed the batter with a steady gaze and waited.

Yeah, let him sweat a bit, I thought.

It seemed like Stewy stood there forever. The batter fidgeted. Stewy released the ball. The batter seemed surprised to see it coming after waiting so long and swung too late.

"Strike one."

The batter threw Stewy a nasty look.

Stewy wiggled his shoulders and arms.

He threw the ball again. This time there was a loud crack as the batter hit it, sending the ball between second and third base. It looked like the guy running to third was sure to score, except the ball took a crazy dive and dropped near the baseline, hitting him in the foot. Automatic out. Two down. One to go.

The batter, who was safe on first, mumbled something about a fluke and gave me a nasty look. The Sabers' coach cursed and threw his hat on the ground. A warning look from the umpire convinced him to pick it up and just mutter under his breath.

The next batter looked a little nervous. I pulled the brim of my cap lower over my eyes and smiled. I bent my knees and punched my glove with my fist. I had never had so much fun at a ball game.

Stewy went into his wind-up and threw. It was high.

"Ball one."

"Like you can, Stewy," Coach Blackmore called and double clapped.

The next pitch was a little wide but the batter swung anyway, getting a piece of it and sending it into foul territory.

"Strike one."

"Come on, batter!" the Sabers' coach yelled. "Don't give them away."

Stewy got into position. Scott held the catcher's mitt open and nodded.

The ball came in just above the batter's knees.

"Strike two!"

"Aw come on, ump!" the Sabers' coach yelled in frustration. The umpire never said a word but just pointed a finger at the coach. This was not a good time to get tossed out of a game, so the coach clammed up.

We didn't dare look at each other. One good hit here and the Sabers could bring in two runs and take the lead. One more strike and the Terriers would win. We had never been so close before. The air crackled with tension.

Stewy went into his wind-up and threw the ball.

There was a crack of bat meeting ball. I expected to see it sailing out of the park but the batter had swung under the ball and sent it flying straight up. Scott threw off his catcher's mask and desperately tried to spot the ball in the sunlight above him.

Whack. The ball sat in Scott's glove. Batter out. Game over. Terriers—four. Sabers—three.

After a couple of seconds of silent disbelief, the realization washed over us. We had WON! Every one of us ran screaming to the pitcher's mound and piled on top of Stewy in a sweaty, dusty heap.

"Hey, what do you think this is?" Stewy sputtered from the bottom of the pile. "A hockey game?"

Coach Blackmore came running out to us, beaming. "I KNEW you could do it!"

"You know what this means?" Scott shouted to me over the noise as he climbed off the pile.

"No, what?" I dusted myself off and went over to where Scott was standing.

"We got statistics."

When Stewy finally dug himself out from the bottom of the pile, he walked over to Scott and me at home plate.

"So, this is what winning feels like," he said with a huge smile on his face. He looked around the field like a king surveying his kingdom. I saw his gaze stop at the Sabers' dugout. Coach Blackmore was shaking the other coach's hand.

The rest of the Terriers brushed themselves off and came over.

"You, um, said something about sending letters for free," Stewy said casually.

"Yeah. Why?"

"'Cuz I'm back in, that's why," Stewy said. "They're not stealing my coach without a fight."

"I'm in, too," Sophie said. The others nodded.

"All right then," I said, unable to keep my smile hidden. "Meet me at the bleachers tomorrow after supper."

June 24, 20-

Edward Heath, President
Harmony Community Centre
Harmony Point, ON
N1S 7C3

THE LOTTERY
FOUNDATION

Dear Mr. Heath,

This is to inform you of our decision regarding the grant request made on behalf of the Harmony Point Community Centre.

For the past eleven years The Lottery Foundation has improved many communities through its Development and Restructuring Grant Program. Last year alone, over 300 million dollars went to support hospitals, seniors' centres, cemeteries and special events such as the Bennington Bull Bonanza.

While it may seem to some that smaller settlements' needs are often overlooked, we wish to assure you of our continued support for communities of all sizes.

Therefore it is with great pleasure that I can inform you that your grant request has been approved. Please find enclosed a cheque for $12,500 to be used to erect a new playground system in Bluffton Park in Harmony Point.

We wish a speedy recovery to all the children suffering from tetanus from the previous rusty play structure.

Sincerely,

Hugh Johnson
Hugh Johnson
Foundation Director

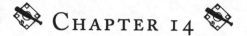

When Scott and I got to the park, the team was already there, sprawled on the bleachers and lying on the grass.

"Geez, you'd think that with school out you'd have a bit more energy," Scott said to them.

"It's the first full day of summer vacation," Tom said. "We need to build up our strength."

"Shouldn't we do something to celebrate?" I asked.

"We are," Stewy said. "We're doing *nothing*. That's something."

I didn't even try and follow Stewy's logic.

"Did you really get the Lottery Foundation to pay for a new climber, Scott?" Sophie asked, looking at the metal dome.

Scott nodded. "I told them that tetanus kills 500,000 people each year and that we've been worried about our playground equipment because it's getting so rusty."

"And they bought that?" Stewy asked, shaking his head.

"Numbers don't lie," Scott said, smiling. "I just didn't tell them that out of the half million cases each year, only about four are in this country."

"You know," Stewy said thoughtfully, "I could see you as an accountant in a major corporation some day."

I took a seat on the bleachers and looked at the old climber. You hardly see those sorts of climbers anymore. We had had some pretty wild games of dome tag on it. I was gonna miss the old dome.

"I heard that Coach Blackmore was checking out the job situation out west," Tim said.

I shuddered. I hoped we weren't already too late.

"So what's the plan, Clay?" Stewy asked finally. Ever since the game, I had tried to come up with some ideas to get things moving faster. We were running out of time.

"We need to get more answers per letter," I said. "It's just taking too long one letter at a time."

"In some of my Mom's magazine, you can ask other readers for recipes and craft ideas," Scott said. "It says some questions get hundreds of answers."

"You been reading your mom's magazines again?" Tom joked.

Scott hit him in the shoulder. "I was looking for letter ideas."

"Recipes, eh? I'll take that," Stewy volunteered. "Maybe I can get some new fudge recipes for my mom. I love fudge."

"And I could ask for quilt patterns for my aunt," Sophie added.

"There's this website called seriouslydudeitsallforfree. com where you can get them to send you free samples and coupons and stuff," Sheldo said, looking excited.

"That's a great idea," Clay said. "Just make sure you order one coupon at a time to get as much mail coming as possible."

"What about those free letters?" Tim asked.

"Oh, yeah. I found out that you don't need a stamp when you write to the government. I got a list of all the Members of Parliament on the internet. We could each take a different one. Tim, how about you take the Minister of Transportation?"

"What should I say? I don't even drive. Well, not, um, *legally*."

"Say something about how the gravel shoulders are all overgrown with weeds. Stuff like that."

"I'm on it."

"Tom, how about the Minister of the Environment? You could complain about all the garbage in Bluffton Creek or about how the widening of the highway to the city destroyed all the trees that used to line the road. Say that the cerulean warbler bird Miss Apfelbaum is so excited about doesn't have anywhere to nest. The Ministry of the Environment loves disasters like that."

"They'll be crying real tears when they finish reading my letter," Tom said.

"Sophie, how about you tackle the Heritage Minister? There's got to be some old building with an interesting history. Maybe we can ask for a historic plaque or something."

"I'll do some research," she said.

"The rest of us can divide up the other MPs and bombard them with questions. We can pretend we're doing a civics project and need information."

"What are these?" Stewy asked, pointing to a pile of cards beside me.

"These are offers to send people a free sample magazine," I said. "I found them in some of the magazines at the grocery store in the city."

"Look, you don't need no stamps on them either," Tim said scanning two or three.

"You don't need *any* stamps, dork," Tom rolled his eyes.

"That's what I just said." Tim stood up. "Don't start with the 'final jeopardy' speech again," he warned, his hand tightening into a fist.

I jumped up too, trying to head off another fight between the twins. Movement at the other end of the park caught my eye. "Hey, isn't that Coach Blackmore walking over there by the creek?"

Stewy jumped down from the bleachers to take a closer look.

"Who's that walking with him?" he asked.

"It looks like," I squinted, "Miss Apfelbaum!"

"Am I just imagining it," Stewy was almost whispering, "or are they holding hands?"

As the path turned to follow the creek, we could see them from behind—and the answer was an obvious *yes*. Stewy stepped back in horror.

"Oh, man!" Stewy wailed, "Could things possibly get any worse?"

"You're overreacting, Stew," I said. "They're adults after all. Hey, maybe they'll get married!"

Stewy grabbed my shirt with both fists, his frightened eyes inches from my face. "Don't you understand? If we lose Coach Blackmore..." he gulped, "we'll lose Miss Apfelbaum, too. And her danish!"

There was a collective gasp. Stewy was right. As impossible as it seemed, things were even worse than we thought.

July 6, 20-

Miss Sophie Williamson
22 Oakridge Drive
Harmony Point, ON
N1S 5D2

Dear Miss Williamson,

Under the Heritage Act you may apply for a Heritage
Designation for any building that has an architectural or
historical significance.

The "really old" post office in Harmony Point may or may not
qualify. Please complete the application we are enclosing and
send it along with any historical documents or pictures that may
assist us in making a decision.

Once the Heritage Advisory Committee makes its
recommendation, it will present it to the Planning Committee.
The Planning Committee will then inform the Regional
Council, who would then inform you.

Thank you for your interest in preserving our heritage.

Very truly yours,

David Delany

David Delany
Architectural Advisor
Special Projects

CHAPTER 15

"**B**ack to work guys. And girl," Coach Blackmore called out from behind the backstop. "Let's warm up those arms."

The end-of-season finals were only two weeks away and Coach Blackmore had us practicing twice a week. All Coach Blackmore's drills were really paying off. We weren't an 'insta-win' for the other team when they played us, and we hadn't been mercied in weeks.

"Okay, team," Coach Blackmore said. "Today we're going to practice hitting the cut-off man."

We were all pretty quiet.

"I don't know, Coach," Stewy finally spoke up, "Last time I hit someone, I was thrown out of the game."

"No, Stewy," Coach Blackmore said. "'Hitting the cut-off man' means throwing the ball to him."

"I don't think we have a cut-off man," Tim said.

Coach Blackmore sighed. "The cut-off man is any infielder between an outfielder and home plate. I want you guys to practice throwing to the cut-off man instead of trying to throw home."

"Why?" Scott asked. I was glad he spoke up, because

I didn't want to look like the only one who had never heard of this.

"It keeps the runners from advancing, which makes it harder for them to score. And it's an easier throw to make. So instead of throwing it all the way to Stewy or Scott and probably missing them, the outfielders can throw to Tim or Tom or Sophie in the infield. And even if the other team gets on base, at least they'll probably have to stop at first or second. And the guy heading for home might think twice."

Coach had four of us in the infield and four in the outfield. Stewy was going to hit some pop flies. Coach had also grabbed the empty garbage can from the play area and laid it on its side at home plate.

"Okay, let's see the outfielders hit the cut-off man and the cut-off throw home. Try and get the ball into the garbage can so we can get used to throwing low so the catcher has a chance to get some guys out sliding home."

Where did he come up with these ideas?

Getting that ball in the garbage can was nearly impossible. It seemed to go everywhere except into the can.

"Look before you throw, Clay," he told me. "Let the ball follow your eyes. You're looking at Stewy instead of the can, which is why you nearly beaned him twice."

"Yeah, Clay. There's no bulls-eye on my helmet, you know," Stewy said.

I tried what Coach said but I never did get a ball in there. I hit the side of the can a couple of times, though, so that was something.

After the practice there was the usual white cardboard box. It used to be a feeding frenzy with all of us grabbing at the danish, but lately we had been taking them out slowly and almost sadly.

"You never know when it could be your last," Stewy whispered to me as he lifted his out of the box with two hands, looked at it from all sides, and then took a big bite and closed his eyes to savour it.

I looked at my own danish long and hard. It was golden brown and totally stuffed with cherry filling, and the gooey white icing swirled over the top and down the sides a bit. If we had to lose something else, why couldn't it be cabbage rolls?

As we were packing up to go, Coach Blackmore handed Sophie a heavy cardboard box. "Here, Sophie. You were asking for old documents and pictures about the town, right? Mrs. Stanfield left this stuff behind in an old storage closet when she moved."

"Thanks, Coach," Sophie said, rifling through faded brown pictures, old ledgers, and personal papers.

"What are you going to do with it all?" Scott asked her.

"The Heritage Ministry is asking for more information on the history of the post office," she answered. "I think we have a good shot at a historic plaque. I just need to fill out an application and send in whatever documents I can find."

"Look, here's someone's journal," Stewy said pulling a leather-bound notebook out of the box. It was worn at the edges and the ink had faded to yellow making it hard to read. As he flipped through the pages a picture fell out and landed at my feet.

"Hey, who's this?" I asked, picking up the picture of an unsmiling woman in a long dress in front of the post office.

We all crowded around. The woman looked hard and determined with strong arms and steely eyes.

"That must be Old Pearl," Stewy said, studying the picture. "My dad told me about her."

"She looks scary," Tim said.

She sure did. I don't know why nobody ever smiled in those old pictures. Maybe they all had bad teeth or something. But it was more than not smiling that made Old Pearl look scary. There was something in the way her eyes stared into the camera.

"There are all kinds of stories about her," Tom said. "They say she kept a loaded shotgun behind the counter and wore men's pants under her skirt."

"Bet she wouldn't let some big shot from the city force her out of *her* job," Stewy said.

I had to agree.

July 14, 20-

Mr. Thomas Steele
37 Parkside Ave.
Harmony, ON
N1S 9C2

Dear Mr. Steele,

This is to confirm that we have received your letter concerning the alleged sighting of a Cerulean Warbler in the north end of Harmony Point. The Cerulean Warbler is indeed on the endangered species list for this jurisdiction and I assure you we take our role in protecting our native species very seriously.

A team will be dispatched shortly to confirm the sighting and investigate the possible destruction of their nesting site. In accordance with ordinance 56.34, subsection 2.4, the expansion of neighbouring urban centres into the suspected warbler range will be halted until a full investigation can be conducted.

Thank you for helping to protect our wildlife.

Samuel Thorne
Samuel Thorne
Assistant to Assistant Deputy Director Willis

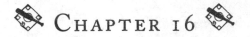

"Who are all those guys over there?" Scott asked, pointing to the far side of the park by Bluffton Creek.

We stopped our warmup and stared. One guy was taking water samples and six others with binoculars were creeping in the bushes and climbing the trees.

"Oh, I bet they're the team from the Ministry of the Environment," Tom said. "I forgot to show you guys my letter." He pulled a crumpled paper out of his back pocket.

"They called you 'Mister'?" Stewy snorted.

"Hey, it was an awesome letter. I used my thesaurus and everything," Tom folded his arms.

"So does this mean the city can't build any closer to Harmony Point?" Sophie asked.

"I think so," Tom said. "At least we won't be swallowed up by the city for a while."

Coach Blackmore called us to the bench to give us our positions and we took the field. This was our second-last game in the regular season and we played hard against the Tigers.

We lost. But even the loss wasn't as bad as before. We

got five solid runs in, and the Tigers never had a chance to mercy us even once. When Stewy had come up to bat their coach yelled, "Back up outfielders. Show some respect."

Stewy looked at our bench like he wondered if this was some kind of joke. There was no spitting, no sneers, and no comments about living in 'the pits.' It was almost as if the Tigers thought we were real competition. The same thing happened at our Saturday game against the Hornets. It ended in a tie.

"Do you think we have a shot at the championship?" I asked Scott the next morning as we sat in our usual spot on the stone wall across the street from the post office.

"Well, even though we ended the season with a couple of wins and a tie, the beginning was so bad that our average still puts us in the basement as far as league standings go," Scott said.

"So, we'll probably have to play the top team in the playoffs then—the Sabers," I said gloomily. "That's going to be a tough game."

"Yeah, but we beat them once, remember? We could do it again."

"I hope so. I don't think I can stand another year of standing on the grass in the outfield with all the other loser teams at the awards presentation."

"Yeah, me neither," he said, shuddering with me at the thought of having to watch as the top three teams lined up around home plate and down the first and third baselines to receive their medals.

"I'd say the odds are 86 to 1 that we make it onto the gravel," Scott said.

I wasn't sure if that was good or bad and didn't really want to ask.

Soon Stewy joined us on the wall. It became almost a ritual each morning for most of us to be across the street from the post office when the delivery truck came.

When we started "Operation Tennis Elbow," as Stewy called it, the truck only dropped off two small bundles of mail wrapped in an elastic band. Then it went up to four bundles, then five.

One day the driver hauled in a full canvas bag of mail. That was the day Stewy celebrated by bringing some maple pecan swirl fudge to practice. So far, Stewy's mom had collected 157 new fudge recipes, and we sure were happy to be the official taste testers.

I was worried, though, that one bag of mail still wasn't enough. I suggested that we double our recipe questions, government queries, and free-magazine requests. A week later, two bags were dropped off. It was time for more fudge.

I also figured it was time to check in with Coach Blackmore and see what he thought. I left most of the team sitting on the wall while I wandered over to the Post Office.

"Looks like this place is pretty busy," I said, very casually.

"Some days I can barely keep up," he admitted. That was the best news I had heard in weeks. I rushed outside to tell the guys.

Stewy lumbered up to the wall a few minutes later, huffing and puffing. "Hey, looks like another victory for Operation Tennis Elbow," he said.

"What are you talking about, Stew?" I asked.

"Follow me." He took off so fast we didn't have time to argue.

We groaned as we hopped off the wall and tagged along behind him. He wouldn't tell us where we were going but had us cut behind Swenson's Hardware Store and then through the hay field until we were almost heading out of town.

"I'm not going one more step until you tell us where you're taking us," Tim yelled from the back of the pack.

Stewy stopped. "Right here."

"Right where?" I asked. We were standing on the gravel shoulder of Highway 51.

Stewy grinned and pointed.

At first I didn't see it. I mean, most of the time I avoided looking at the town sign because it made me want to hit something. So it took a second to sink in that the sign had been fixed.

"I saw it when we drove back from the city yesterday," Stewy said.

'HARMONY POINT' stood out in crisp white letters. All twelve letters. And it hadn't just been repainted, either. It was a whole new sign on brand new wooden posts.

It was a work of art. I don't think that even the Mona Lisa could look better than our new sign. We cheered and high-fived each other. It felt like things were finally turning around.

"Do you think someone'll just wreck it again?" Tom asked.

My heart sank. I hadn't even thought of that. What if vandals came along and did it again?

"We need to protect it," Tim said.

"How?" Scott asked. "It's not like we can stand guard over it day and night."

"It's probably safe until next April Fool's Day, anyway," I said. "That gives us almost a full year to prove to everyone that Harmony Point *isn't* the armpit of the region."

"How do we do that?" Stewy asked.

"We win."

July 17, 20-

Mrs. Dana Krakowski
67 Walter Street
Harmony Point, ON
N1S 4C9

Dear Mrs. Krakowski,

How excited I was to read that you were looking for fudge recipes!
I have won the Rockwood Agricultural Fair's red ribbon for this
fudge seven years in a row. As the judges decided I was no longer
allowed to enter this particular fudge in the fair, I am thrilled to
share it with you. I know in my heart that my delicious fudge
could not have been the cause of Judge Silvano's diabetes.

FANTASY FUDGE

Ingredients:

3 cups sugar	1 200g jar marshmallow cream
¾ cup butter	1 cup chopped walnuts
1 160 ml can evaporated milk	1 teaspoon vanilla
1 350g pkg semi-sweet chocolate chips	

Combine sugar, butter and milk in a 2L (8 cup) saucepan; bring
to a boil, stirring constantly. Continue boiling 5 minutes over
medium heat, stirring constantly (mixture scorches easily).

Remove from heat; stir in choc chips until melted. Add
marshmallow cream, nuts and vanilla. Beat until well-blended.
Pour into a greased 13" x 9" pan. Cool.

Enjoy!

Edith Kovacs

 CHAPTER 17

It was only two days later when we were at our usual post on the stone wall that we saw Mr. Canada Post arrive.

He was easy to recognize. He carried a briefcase and wore a suit. Nobody wore a suit on a Wednesday morning in Harmony.

"What do we do?" Scott asked as we watched through the window as Coach Blackmore shook the guy's hand.

"Wait until he's gone and then go in and act surprised at the good news," I answered. All our hard work was about to pay off.

Mr. Canada Post seemed to be there for a long time. As we waited, the delivery truck pulled up and the driver hauled two and a half canvas bags inside.

We cheered. That was sure to clinch it. Not even Canada Post could deny that Harmony needed a post office now.

As soon as Mr. Canada Post left, Scott and I went in to see Coach Blackmore to get the good news. He was holding on to the counter with both hands as if he needed to keep himself upright.

"Hi, Coach," Scott said.

Coach Blackmore jumped. "Hi, guys." He smiled weakly.

We looked at each other in alarm. Coach Blackmore looked much more upset than we would have expected, considering we had just saved his job.

"Who was that man?" Scott asked innocently.

"Oh, that was my supervisor from Canada Post."

"What did he want?" I asked, wondering why Coach Blackmore was trembling.

"They have been checking into some things, working some numbers."

"Well," I said, "What did he say? How were your numbers?"

"Much worse than expected, I'm sorry to say."

"*What?*" Scott and I blurted out at the same time.

"But you said that you had so much mail coming in you could hardly keep up," I said. I was sure I had heard wrong.

"Oh, I do. It's almost more than I can handle."

"Then, the number of letters coming through still isn't high enough?" Scott asked.

Mr. Blackmore looked confused. "There's more than enough mail coming in. That's not the problem."

Now Scott and I were confused.

"The problem is renovating this building. This old place needs a lot of repairs, the roof, the plumbing, the furnace, new wiring, a sprinkler system. It's a long list and the post office has been running the numbers of the cost to bring it up to code. They think it would be cheaper in the long run to just move this station to the city."

I couldn't even answer. It was all a bad dream. Was he really telling us that it had never been about the amount of mail coming through? That all our letter writing was for nothing?

We trudged outside to break the news to the others.

"So you're telling me we didn't need to write no letters?" Tim asked, his face tight.

"We didn't need to write *any* letters," Tom said and ducked Tim's punch.

"I knew it," Stewy said. "This whole thing was a waste of time and paper."

I felt too miserable to even answer.

"Not really," Sophie said. We all looked at her. "Some good things came out of it, right?"

"Sure," Stewy said, folding his arms. "I can name every minister in the current government. I should ace next year's Social Studies."

Everyone chuckled.

Sophie stuck her chin out. "We got new uniforms, didn't we?"

"It *is* kind of nice to look like a team," I admitted.

"And a new playground?"

A few people shuffled their feet.

"Yeah, and Miss Apfelbaum got a concussion," Stewy said sarcastically.

"She got a signed picture of her idol," Sophie said.

"I heard she sleeps with it on her pillow," Scott whispered to me. We stifled our laughs when we saw Sophie's face.

"It's not every town that can stop a megacity from creeping up on its borders," she said.

"I guess it *is* good that the forest between us and the city is now protected for the cerulean warbler and we won't be surrounded by mini malls," Scott said.

"And we got a new town sign," she added.

"No more ARM P I T," I said and couldn't help smiling.

"We accomplished a *lot*," she said.

"Still," Stewy said. "It didn't save Coach Blackmore's job."

No one had an answer to that.

July 20, 20-

Fringe Magazines

Mr. Sheldon Rose
45 Parkside Avenue
Harmony Point, ON
N1S 9C2

Dear Mr. Rose,

We are pleased to send you your free trial issue of our magazine *On Board!* We hope that you will find it entertaining and informative whether you snow, skate or wake board. This month's in-depth feature, "Wax On, Wax Off" is sure to improve your skill.

While we have your attention, we thought we would let you know about some other fine magazines we offer through our company.

Are you hooked on hypotenuses? Do you quiver for quadratic equations? Then let me introduce you to *It's as Easy as Pi*, the magazine for those of you who are mad for math. Each month we'll feature a *world famous* mathematician and the number problem that brought him to his knees.

Into more hands-on projects? Join in the popular cheese-sculpting craze. *Cut the Cheese* gives you exclusive articles on timely subjects such as, *"Do you Know Where Your Colby has Been?"* and *"Eat your Mistakes."*

As you can see, we have magazines for every interest. Please let your family, friends, neighbours, co-workers, sports teams, church groups and local politicians know about us. <u>We look forward to your order.</u>

Sincerely,

Dom Fraser

Dom Fraser
Executive Editor
Fringe Magazines

"Three up, three down" was not the way we had wanted to start the first inning of the end-of-season league championships. Stewy, Sophie, and I were the first three in the Terriers' batting order and we each had come up to bat, struck out, and sat back down on the bench. It had taken all of seven minutes.

When the Sabers came to bat, they mercied us. We knew it wouldn't be easy facing the first place team, but geez, what a lousy first inning. After their six runs came in, I saw the Sabers high-five each other and agree how lucky they were to draw us for their first round-robin game. They figured it would be an easy win. You know, maybe they were right. Maybe *loser* was the right label for us after all.

Stewy slid over to me on the bench. "So," he asked, "did you call?"

All eyes turned to me. "Yeah, I called."

"Well? What did they say?" Stewy asked. We had all agreed that the time had come for a call directly to Canada Post. Seeing as this was all my idea to begin with, I got elected to try and beg for the survival of our post office. It wasn't what I'd call, you know, *successful*.

"When I finally got to talk to someone, they said they had nothing more to do with it and I should talk to some other government guy," I said.

"What does *that* mean?" Tim asked.

"That means they're passing the buck about closing the post office," I said, folding my arms. "The same thing happened to my dad when he complained about our taxes. No one wants to take responsibility for any problems so they transfer you from ministry to ministry until you've told your story to everyone from the Department of Fisheries to the Minister of Public Safety. In the end, the result will be the same—no post office and no baseball coach."

"And no danish," Stewy said, choking back a sob.

Coach Blackmore came over to the bench, his forehead wrinkled. "Come on Terriers. Let's see some energy out there." He lifted the white cardboard box. "How about some danish?"

The sight of the box only made us more depressed. No one could bring themselves to take one.

Well, the second inning was different from the first, all right. This time it only took the Sabers six minutes to have us go three up, three down. And then they mercied us again.

"Twelve to nothing," I said to no one in particular. Even Scott didn't want to hear *those* numbers.

"We might as well line up in the outfield right now," Stewy said, throwing his glove on the ground.

"Come on, Terriers! Where's that fire you had in you the last few games?" Coach Blackmore asked. "We need a big inning here. Tim, you're up. Tom you're on deck. Let's keep that bat level and put some *umpf* behind it." He double clapped as Tim lugged the bat to the plate. Didn't look like there was any fire in Tim.

We tried to battle, we really did, but by the fifth inning the score was 16 to 1 and the ten-run rule meant that the game was over. You know, it was almost a relief. Sometimes it's just easier to let things stay the way they are.

Coach Blackmore called us all together on the field after the game. "What happened guys? And girl?" I watched him look around at all the blank eyes and drooping shoulders. "You've all worked so hard this year but it's like you forgot everything we've practiced. It's like I had never coached you at all."

I saw the disappointed expression on Coach Blackmore's face. Suddenly, I realized—*we* were used to losing but *he* wasn't. I felt horrible that we had let him down. I sure didn't want him to think that all the work he did in his only season with us was for nothing. He deserved a better effort from us.

"I'm sorry, Coach," I said. "We'll try harder." I looked at the others.

"Yeah, we're real sorry," Stewy said.

Coach Blackmore smiled. "We're not out of this yet, you know. We have two more games tomorrow. But we've got to show them what we're made of."

We met at the ball diamond in the town of Alma the next morning for our second round-robin game. The Pirates were already there, warming up and looking awfully confident. They must have heard about our first game. Well, we were determined that it wasn't going to be an easy win for them today.

Coach Blackmore drove up a few minutes late. He carried a brown cardboard box in one arm and waved us over with his other. He had a big smile on his face, like he didn't have a care in the world, which was odd for a guy who had just lost his job.

"Shoes off, guys and girl," he said, grinning. He reached into the box and pulled out ten pairs of real baseball socks. You know—those white knit socks that are long enough to reach your knees. Ours had green stripes down the outside to match our jerseys.

"Wow, these are great!" I said. It's amazing how a real uniform can make you feel like a real ball player.

Coach Blackmore smiled at the excitement on our

faces. "Okay Terriers, now let's see you get them dirty!" He double clapped and sent us back to our warm-up.

I was never sure whether it was the socks or just all of us wanting to see Coach Blackmore proud of us, but we ended up tying the Pirates. It was a tough game from the start, but things began to turn around when Stewy got a monster hit in the fifth inning to get two runs in. And Sophie tied it up in the seventh when she got a single and then stole her way around the bases. We were on our feet screaming when the guy on third fumbled the catch that would have got her out and she took off for home. The guy on third was so rattled that he threw way too high and the catcher didn't stand a chance of getting it. He watched sourly as Sophie slid neatly into home plate.

"Good work, Terriers!" Coach Blackmore high-fived everyone as we came off the field. "Let's keep it up for our next game this afternoon."

"What time do we need to be back here?" I asked.

"Well, I thought it would be a good idea if we stayed here together as a team over lunch," he said. "So if some of you guys give me a hand, I have my portable barbeque in the trunk of my car. We can set up over there under the trees."

Tim grabbed the barbeque and the rest of us helped Coach Blackmore pull bags of food and plates and napkins and coolers out of his car.

"Be sure and thank your parents," Coach Blackmore said. "They thought it was a great idea when I mentioned it and have sent a ton of food."

"This is AWESOME!" Stewy said, drooling at the sight of hamburgers, hot dogs, chips, ice-cold drinks and a huge watermelon.

"Oh, and Miss Apfelbaum sent these," Coach Blackmore said as his blush spread from his ears all the way down his neck. He opened two huge white cardboard boxes stuffed with danish. "She thought you needed some energy."

I think the danish must have worked its magic.

Stewy pitched like a major leaguer and we held the Tigers to four runs. He also smacked a beautiful double to drive Sophie and Tom in for a two runs in the second inning and Scott got home on a steal in the fourth. Tim and I made it home in the sixth to end the game—five to four for us.

You know, the feeling of winning never got old.

After the game, everyone crowded around the concession booth where the team standings were posted on a huge whiteboard.

"How far down are we?" Stewy asked me. I was balanced on his shoulders to see over the crowd of players.

"The Sabers are first with five points," I said. "Looks like they had two wins and a tie. The Pirates are next with one win and two ties for four points."

"Clay, start at the bottom. It'll be faster and you're getting heavy," Stewy grunted.

"Wait," I pushed down on Stewy's head to try and get higher. "It can't be."

"Can't be what?" Stewy asked.

"We're tied for third with three points!" I said and then hit the ground with a thump as Stewy dumped me and pushed his way forward through the crowd to see for himself.

It was true. Both the Hornets and Tigers did worse than we did. The Hornets tied twice for two points and the Tigers were in the basement with only one point.

The Sabers and Pirates would play for first and second place and we would meet the Bulldogs to play for third place. The Terriers versus the Bulldogs game was the talk of the tournament. They all started calling it the 'Dog Fight.'

I had never even imagined that we would play in the finals. I was almost afraid to believe it.

"This is for the gravel or the grass," I said to Stewy.

"Geez, the stakes don't get any higher than that, do they?" he said.

"Better tell Miss Apfelbaum to start baking," I said.

July 22, 20-

Mr. Stewy Scott
6 Third Avenue
Harmony Point, ON
N1S 4J2

Dear Mr. Scott,

It is not often that we get requests for information about the Privy Council Office, so we were delighted to send you lots of material on our function and importance in working with the government.

We are sorry to hear that your civics project is finished and that you wish us to "stop sending you stuff." We still have many more files and pamphlets full of interesting facts and figures.

We hope that you will change your mind or begin a new project soon. In the meantime, we will compile a folder of numerous documents and memos. It will be sitting here, ready to Expresspost as soon as you give the word.

Happy to have been of help,

Bill Driver

Bill Driver
Deputy Secretary to the Cabinet,
Legislation & Housing Planning, & Machinery of Government,
Counsel to the Clerk of the Privy Council

CHAPTER 19

We had to wait a whole week to play the finals. We practiced at least three times over the next few days to get ready. Coach Blackmore looked pretty relaxed considering all those men and women in dark suits carrying briefcases that were parading in and out of the post office every day. I couldn't figure out what they were doing there. Wasn't it a bit cruel to remind him every day that his job was gone?

Not one of us on the team could bear to talk about it. We stopped hanging out anywhere near the post office altogether. In fact, if anyone, anywhere, started to say anything at all about Mr. Blackmore or his job, I would leave. It was a pretty sore spot with me, and I know I wasn't the only one on the team to avoid the topic. We also didn't mention the Letter Writing Fiasco, as Stewy now called it.

I did happen to overhear that the date for the Big Move was the Monday after the finals, but I pushed it out of my mind.

The day of the big game, the Bulldogs showed up at Bluffton Park carrying their matching sports bags and jackets. They looked calm, confident, and ready for the Dog Fight.

We leaned our assorted bats against the backstop and put our multi-coloured helmets on the bench. I was already losing my nerve.

Coach Blackmore saw me looking at the Bulldogs. "It's not the equipment that wins the game, Clay," he said. "We just need to play *our* game. Shut them down at the plate and find the holes in their defense when we're at bat."

"Yeah," I said, watching the batters warm up with their portable batting cage. "Nothing to it."

A small car skidded to a stop in the parking lot. Out popped Miss Apfelbaum, carrying her trademark white cardboard box. Coach Blackmore was blushing before she even reached the dugout.

"Oh, thank goodness," she said. "I thought I was late. Stewy, how's your pitching arm?"

"Pretty good, I think," he said, swinging it in wide circles.

"Good. Well, I'll leave this box here if anyone needs a boost of energy." She beamed at Coach Blackmore and went to find a seat on the bleachers.

As the home team, we were in the field first. The Bulldogs got a couple of hits but left the runners stranded as Tom caught a pop fly and two batters struck out.

We went three up, three down. Not a good start, you know.

Then the Bulldogs went three up, three down. I didn't even know we could do that to another team. It was the bottom of the second inning with no score.

"Okay, team." Coach Blackmore double clapped as Tim went up to bat. "Let your bats do the talking."

It seemed to all come together then. For the next five innings we battled back and forth with the Bulldogs. We got some solid hits to bring in four runs. One of them was even thanks to me. Tim got home and Sophie made it to third on the line drive I got when I remembered to keep my swing level.

"Hey, way to move them around, Clay," Scott said to me when I jogged back after being thrown out at first. "Two runs in!"

"It was only one run, Scott. What's happened to your math?"

Scott just grinned at me. "Are you kidding? Sophie's now on third. Do you really think they stand a chance of holding her there?"

They didn't. A pop fly by Sheldo into right field was all she needed. The second that ball hit the outfielder's glove, she was off like a rocket. I don't think he even realized what was happening until she was halfway to home plate. She didn't even bother to slide.

We were feeling pretty good after that until Stewy ran into a little pitching trouble in the sixth inning. Before you could say "cherry danish" the Bulldogs had tied the game and had the bases loaded with only one out. I was afraid Stewy was going to fall apart. I knew he desperately wanted to finish the game and was constantly looking to see if Dale was warming up in the bullpen.

But Coach Blackmore didn't seem worried. "Like you can, Stewy," he called out and double clapped.

Stewy settled down then and struck the next two batters out. He came off the field with a huge grin on his face.

But we still had a big job ahead of us. We had to keep the Bulldogs from earning any more runs in the seventh and we then had to score ourselves. I got a little worried when the Bulldogs managed to get a runner on third. Okay, a lot worried. When his teammate hit the ball and he started for home, I imagined the worst.

Sanjay ran full out to get to the ball and threw right to the cutoff. Tom relayed it to Scott at home plate. That ball came in so fast and low that Scott was able to catch it right about the bag and make the tag in time. It was an awesome play. We were pumped.

"Hey, who's that coming in to pitch?" Stewy asked, seeing a new Bulldog warming up on the mound.

I felt my blood run cold. It was the Shinbuster. I prayed that someone in the lineup before me would score a run before I had to come up to bat.

Tom was first up but struck out. Stewy was up next. The Bulldogs weren't taking any chances with him. They gave him an intentional walk to first, knowing they had a better chance of throwing him out than catching one of his monster hits.

Sophie had a beautiful single but was thrown out trying to stretch it out to a double. Still, Stewy had made it to third base.

I was up. I swallowed hard. It was the bottom of the seventh, with two out and a tie game. All I had to do was get a hit and bring Stewy home.

The pitcher went into his wind-up.

I had to jump back as the ball whistled past my knees.

"Strike one!"

"Okay, Clay. You've had a look at it now," Coach Blackmore called.

The next pitch was even faster and closer to my knees.

"Strike two!"

"Come on, Clay. Protect the plate now, buddy."

I stretched my shoulders, which were tight with tension.

"Bring me home, Clay!" Stewy called from third. Yeah, like I needed more pressure.

I could feel the sweat beading on my forehead. I knew the next pitch was coming straight for my shins.

"Play's to first, boys," the Bulldogs' coach called to his team, holding up his index finger. "Forget about the guy on third. Let's get the batter."

The ball came screaming at me at about a hundred miles an hour. I never took my eyes off it. I felt the vibration all the way up my arms when the bat connected with the ball. It was a beautiful line drive that skimmed the ground just past the short stop.

I took off for first. Stewy took off for home.

The centrefielder ran for the ball and stooped to pick it up. I saw him hesitate for a second. He was supposed to throw to first but I was almost at the bag and Stewy was lumbering only halfway home. Stewy looked like a sure out.

The centrefielder couldn't resist. He made a huge throw to home. The catcher wasn't expecting the throw and had to bolt forward to get the ball, which bounced on the ground a few feet in front of him.

He grabbed the ball and ran to tag Stewy.

"Slide, Stewy! Slide!" yelled Coach Blackmore.

Stewy dropped down only a few feet from home plate and slid feet-first with his arms in the air.

The catcher's glove hit Stewy's thigh a full second before his foot slid over home plate.

The Bulldogs started cheering. Stewy stood up and stomped on home plate in anger.

"SAFE!" the umpire called, his arms straight out to either side. "Safe!" he repeated.

The Bulldogs' coach, parents, and players erupted into a near riot. You should have heard them.

"Are you *insane*, ump?" the Bulldogs' coach roared over the yelling.

Coach Blackmore looked at our fans in the bleachers and shrugged. Everyone in the park had seen the tag before Stewy reached home plate.

The umpire pulled off his mask and put his hands on his hips, feet spread.

The Bulldogs' coach tore over to him, his face purple with rage. "He tagged him *miles* from the plate! He should be out!" he screamed.

"And he would *be* out," the umpire said calmly, folding his arms, "if he had tagged him with the *ball*."

Every head in the park swiveled to the catcher who stood forlornly, looking down at the ball in his right hand and the empty glove in his left.

The umpire threw both hands up in the air, "That's the game!" he said and walked off the field.

I turned to Scott, stunned and amazed. We had done it. We had come back from being the worst team in history to winning third place and a spot on the gravel at the awards ceremony. There wasn't a word strong enough to describe how it felt.

An hour later, my sneakers crunched on the gravel as I lined up with Coach Blackmore and the rest of the Terriers along the third baseline.

I smiled at Scott beside me. Scott grinned at Stewy. Stewy nudged Sophie. Sophie winked at the twins.

After saying a few words, the league convener placed the medals around each of our necks.

"It's just like the Olympics, man," Stewy whispered, practically trembling.

I ran my fingers over the back of his medal where the words "Third Place, Peewee Intercounty Championship" and the date were engraved.

After the other two teams got their medals, I turned to Coach Blackmore beside me and stuck out my hand. "Thanks for everything, Coach," I said.

The rest of the team crowded around. Everyone shook Coach Blackmore's hand and Sophie gave him a hug. I didn't mention to anyone that Coach Blackmore's eyes looked misty.

From: Jean Stanfield [jstanfield@supernet.ca]
To: William Blackmore [harmony.point@canadapost.gc.ca]

Subject: Congratulations, Terriers!!

Mr. Blackmore and the whole Terriers team:

I was thrilled to hear of your third place victory! Congratulations to everyone.
Miss you all! Wish I could be there to celebrate. ☹

Jean Stanfield

P.S. Could you courier me a piece of cake?

CHAPTER 20

The next night, a big party was planned for us in Bluffton Park. Maybe we failed to save our post office and our coach, but at least for once the village had won something. It had been a long time since Harmony could celebrate a victory—any victory.

The afternoon before the party the whole team met across the street from the post office and watched through the window as Mr. Blackmore packed everything in boxes.

"We should help him," Sophie said. "We are his team, even if it was for only one season."

"Yeah, let's go pitch in," I said. We walked across the street and went inside.

Mr. Blackmore smiled at us. "Hi, guys and girl."

"Hi Coach," Tim said. "We just thought we'd give you a hand."

"Well, that's great. You guys can start taking these boxes."

"Sure," Stewy said, helping some of the guys with the heavier ones. "So when does the moving van get here?"

Mr. Blackmore smiled again. "I don't need a van to move down the street, Stewy."

Six boxes dropped on the ground.

"You're moving down the street?" I could hardly process the words in my brain.

"Sure. Well, temporarily." He saw the confused look on my face. "It should only take a few months." He said it like that should explain it. I still had no idea what he was talking about.

"*What* should only take a few months?" Scott was the first to find his voice.

"The renovations for the post office."

"I thought you said it was going to cost too much?" Stewy said.

"Well, for Canada Post it was. But last week we got notice from the Heritage Ministry that they were getting involved. Seems they've uncovered an amazing history to this place and they want to preserve it as a historic site."

"What's so 'historic' about this old place?" Stewy asked.

"It turns out it's more than just an old post office and stagecoach stop. The whole story came out in a very interesting old journal that was sent to them," Coach Blackmore said.

We all looked at Sophie. Mr. Blackmore followed our stares.

Sophie blushed.

"It was in that box of papers you gave me," she said,

trying to explain without giving away the whole Letter Writing Fiasco. "I just thought the Heritage Ministry would be interested."

Mr. Blackmore nodded. "They absolutely love that sort of thing. Especially when it turns out to be the diary of a notorious outlaw, Pearl Hart, who was born only a few miles from here. There always was a bit of a mystery about what happened to her. Seems after she got out of prison, she disappeared. They looked for her for years. Turns out this little post office was her hideout."

"You mean Old Pearl was an outlaw?" Clay asked.

"That's right. I guess no one thought to look for her in Harmony Point," he said with a smile.

"What was she in prison for?" I asked.

"Robbing stagecoaches."

"Cool!" Stewy said.

"Anyway," Coach Blackmore continued, "Once they're done with all the renovations they'll designate this as a heritage site. And since it's not good for an old building to sit empty, they're going to give the post office a break on the rent. So now it's actually cheaper to stay here than to move us to the city. So I'm setting up temporarily in Swenson's Hardware."

"Then…then you're not leaving?" Sophie asked, suddenly realizing what it all meant. "You'll still be our coach?"

"Sure. If you want me to," he blushed slightly.

There was an explosion of cheers as we all laughed. And high-fived each other.

The end-of-the-season celebration in Bluffton Park was the party of the year. It looked like the whole village was there. We posed with Coach Blackmore, wearing our medals for what seemed like a thousand pictures.

When we thought we were finally done, someone shouted, "Wait! Let's have one with the cake!"

Everyone laughed as we stood around the most amazing creation I had ever seen. Miss Apfelbaum had outdone herself.

The bottom was a chocolate cake carved and iced to look just like an open baseball glove. In it sat a perfectly round, white cake baseball. The icing seams made it look almost real. And all over the ball was each Terrier's name autographed in chocolate.

It was a masterpiece.

Beside it sat paper plates, plastic forks, and *Way to Go!* napkins.

"Oh no!" I said laughing. "Not the *Way to Go!* napkins again!"

"Good for any occasion," Scott said, laughing with me.

I was first in line for a piece of the cake. I wanted the one with my name on it. As I munched on my cake, I saw Scott counting heads.

"How many?" I asked him.

"Three hundred and thirty-four," Scott said. "That's over ninety-six percent," he added.

"That's got to be a record," I said.

"Yup," he said. "Of course, you *know* why."

I looked at him, grinning. "Cake?"

"Not just any cake," Scott's smile spread across his whole face. "It's an Apfelbaum."

GLOSSARY OF BASEBALL TERMS

Bunting Deliberately hitting the ball gently by holding the bat still, in front of the batter, and letting the ball hit it so that it rolls a short distance on the ground.

Cut-off man A fielder that 'cuts off' a long throw from the outfield so he can get the ball to a base quickly in order to put out a runner.

Double play A play where two players are put out on one play.

Grounder A ball that is hit on the ground so that it bounces in the infield.

Infield The area on a baseball field that is inside the three bases and home plate.

Inning A period of baseball in which both teams take a turn being up at bat AND playing defense in the field. In the Major Leagues, there are nine innings in a regulation game. In Minor League/ Little League, there are usually only seven innings.

Lead (or lead off) When a base runner takes a step or two off the base before the pitch is thrown so he has a shorter distance to run to the next base.

Line drive A ball hit sharply, low and fast, so that it usually flies in a straight line.

Mercy rule In Little League, this rule ends one team's turn at bat after they have scored a certain number of runs (usually five or six). It can also end the game if one team has scored a certain number of runs more than the other team by the end of the 5th inning.

Outfield   The grassy area of a baseball field past the lines connecting the bases.

Pop fly   A ball that is hit high into the air. If the fielder catches it before it hits the ground, then the runner is out and whoever is already on base has to run back to their bases before they are tagged.

Rundown   A play in which a runner is stranded between two bases, running back and forth, trying not to be tagged with the ball.

Shortstop   The fielder who plays between second and third base.

Tagged   A runner who is touched by a fielder with the ball is tagged out.

To learn more about the rules of baseball,
visit these sites:
Major League Baseball
www.mlb.com
Baseball Canada
www.baseball.ca
Little League Baseball
http://www.littleleague.org/learn/rules.htm

For more information and some fun activities,
visit our website at
www.fitzhenry.ca/savingarmpit